Twists AND Turns

~ Also by Janet McDonald ~

Spellbound
Chill Wind
Brother Hood
Harlem Hustle

Twists and Turns

Janet McDonald

Farrar, Straus and Giroux

Library of Congress Cataloging-in-Publication Data
McDonald, Janet.
   Twists and turns / Janet McDonald.— 1st ed.
     p. cm.
   Summary: With the help of a couple of successful friends, Teesha and Keeba
try to capitalize on their talents by opening a hair salon in the run-down
Brooklyn housing project where they live.
   ISBN-13: 978-0-374-40006-4 (pbk.)
   ISBN-10: 0-374-40006-7 (pbk.)
   1. African Americans—Juvenile fiction. [1. African Americans—Fiction.
2. Public housing—Fiction. 3. Entrepreneurship—Fiction. 4. Sisters—
Fiction. 5. Brooklyn (New York, N.Y.)—Fiction.] I. Title.

PZ7.M4784178 Tw 2003
[Fic]—dc21

2002035313

To Paris, where I became possible

Acknowledgments

Great gratitude for splendid editor Frances Foster and the artful Janine O'Malley, inspiring artist-in-residence Gwen Wock, my witty and courageous brother Kevin, compatriot and *complice* Françoise Greisch, and literary agent Charlotte Sheedy. A wail of shouts to Hawaiian Sunrae, French Colette, Brooklyn Paulie, Kazoo Annie, Canadian Nat, and One Nation Val; hollas to Joey Fury, Rowena Carey, Yakov Golyadkin, gallant Lisa H., TV Mad Stuart, Samuel Barber, Simone *clair de lune*, and to the Gregors, Polly and Samsa.

Twists and Turns

1

Music thumped the walls like fists, pounding inside the Washingtons' apartment. Edwina Percy Washington was away at yet another weekend church function. And once again her daughters hadn't been able to go with her. Cramps, they said. As she always did, Mrs. Washington told them to rest, say their prayers at night, and invite only girls over if they wanted company. And as they often did, Keeba and Teesha said, "Sure, Ma," and threw a loud, boisterous party with boys from all over Hillbrook Houses.

Although a year younger, Teesha had graduated high school right alongside her sister. Teesha herself was a year behind, but Keeba had been held back a couple of grades and was the oldest graduate in the class. You'd never know it from their marks, but the Washington sisters were bright, each in her own way. Teesha liked anything with numbers—math puzzles, arithmetic board games, or just playing with a calculator. Keeba preferred imitating characters she saw on TV and in movies and could repeat their lines by heart. They simply weren't motivated to study, or even to attend class regularly. It was as though something else was beckoning to them. Still, they'd managed to get their diplomas and both of them were proud.

Finishing school wasn't all they were celebrating, though. Their smartest best friend, Raven Jefferson, was home for the summer from college; their nerdiest best friend, Toya Larson, had been accepted into a computer training program; and their overall best friend, Aisha Ingram, was making mad cash doing TV commercials. Hillbrook girls were on a roll.

The living room was bathed in pink from lightbulbs the sisters had colored red with magic markers. On the kitchen table sat Mrs. Washington's new punch bowl, which Keeba had taken from its box and filled with grape Kool-Aid. Around the bowl were placed a half dozen oblong glass platters, dishware their mother said was reserved strictly for church dinners, now piled high with bright orange Cheez Doodles.

Earlier in the day, Teesha had gone to the grocery store to buy food for the party. Determined to stretch the weekend grocery money as far as she could, she saw little sense, once she'd found her favorite item on sale, in buying anything else. Pointing to the expiration date, the cashier had asked if Teesha was sure she wanted the six jumbo-paks. Most definitely, Teesha said. After all, Cheez Doodles didn't get old.

For her part, Keeba had done the cleaning. In a manner of speaking, that is. She threw some water on the dirty dishes, kicked some magazines and newspapers strewn on the floor under the couch, and ran her hand over the furniture, collecting giant fluffy dustballs that she tossed out the window.

The party was pumping. Everybody was in a sweat, even with the windows open, and voices filled the night. People had gathered in a circle as the sisters and their main girls boogied through a series of old-time, played-out dances.

"The Worm!" shouted Keeba, sliding her neck from side to side. Teesha danced over to her sister, mirroring her moves. Then Teesha called for the Bounce. Like a gym class doing shoulder raises, the teens bounced their shoulders up and down in rhythm to Missy Elliott's smooth beats.

"Ah-ight, y'all," shouted Aisha, "check *this* out, the Electric Slide on wheels!"

On her skates, she took three steps to the left and three to the right, leaned backward, then bent forward into a front wheel spin, all without missing a beat. Kids lined up behind her and soon the entire living room was electric-sliding.

"Damn, Aisha, you rock!" exclaimed her ex-boyfriend, Kevin Vinker.

"Nah, brother, she *rules*," said her current boyfriend, Max Payne.

"My girl Ai can do on skates what I can't even do on my feet," said Raven as she stumbled into the forward dip, almost falling. Her fiancé, Jesse Honoré, caught her just in time.

Not to be outdone, since the party was *supposed* to be for her too, Toya broke away from the line dance to do her specialty, the Booty. Rolling her hips back and forth, she eased down in slow motion and rose up again to the chant of "Go, Toya! Go, Toya! Go! Go! Go!"

Bodies rocked and rolled in rhythm, and in the middle of the writhing mass Keeba was working her hips against a boy in an FDNY cap. For the party, Teesha had put a lot of effort into getting Keeba's hair exactly right: braided to the base of her neck, the rest left to hang loose down her back. The boy dancing with her wanted a touch.

"I don't *think* so, Arkim Hamilton. You out your mind? Nobody puts their hands on my hair but my sister," declared Keeba.

"Wassup with that? It ain't like the cowboy never touched that horse's tail."

"What?! No, you *didn't* say my braids came off no horse, Arkvark! This hair is pure human."

Arkim was doubled over laughing.

"You always think you funnier than you ain't," she said.

Keeba swept her hair over one shoulder and walked off. She was laughing too, but she wouldn't let Arkim see her doing it. He was so *stoopid*! A horse! Nobody had invited him anyway. He just always showed up because he lived upstairs.

"Then let me touch that bootylicious," he called after her.

Lately, Keeba had skated less and eaten more than her sister, Teesha, who had transformed her "booty body" into a lean, sexy physique. But Keeba wasn't jealous. If she saw her sister preening at the mirror, she'd push her aside to admire her own image and would break into her favorite line from the Sir Mix-A-Lot rap classic, "Even white boys got to shout, Baby got back!"

It didn't matter that Teesha smirked and said Sir Mix-A-Lot was so *over*. What *did* bother Keeba was when her sister treated her like she was stupid, going "Duh!" every time she said something that might be a little wak. Being older, she wanted her kid sister to look up to and even admire her, at least a little bit. But Teesha *did* take up for her whenever anybody *else* dissed her, which was cool.

Max was deep into Keeba's dance moves. "Don't *hurt* nobody Kee!"

Noticing where Max's eyes were fixed, Aisha snatched him around.

"I'ma hurt *you* in a minute if you don't stop eyeballing

Kee's butt. Remember that movie where the lady poured boiling hot grits on her man because he was creeping with somebody else? Ah-ight then, watch ya back." She kissed his cheek.

Max shook his head. "That wasn't a movie, Ai. That was what really happened to that old R&B singer Al Green."

"Oh yeah, that's right! Well anyway, you better get out the cocoa butter 'cause them grits gon' burn."

Meanwhile, Teesha was getting her own groove on. Dancing in the center of a group, her hair styled by Keeba in a crown of thick, loose twists, Teesha looked very much the part of reigning queen. She gave herself the role of keeping their parties in line and her subjects in order.

A few rude people had something nasty to say about the food, but she let them know straight up where to find the nearest McDonald's. And when a couple of boys complained she never had anything "for the head," she directed them to the bedroom where the pillows were. It was one thing to let people bring their own liquor, but other stuff was too crazy. A lot of kids went downhill fast messing with drugs. And anyway, she wasn't about to give the Housing Authority an excuse to put them out of the projects. Despite the limited munchies and the drug ban, Teesha felt the evening was a hit and that she and her sister were still at the top of the project party scene.

But not everyone was having a good time. An unlikely pair stood next to each other in the kitchen. One of the two, Ashley Honoré, was decked out in a turquoise silk blouse and black silk slacks. A recent graduate from an exclusive women's college on her way to business school, Ashley had never been in the projects before and would have kept it that way had her younger brother, Jesse, not dragged her there. He planned to marry Raven, a Hillbrook girl, and wanted his sister to get over her snobbery issues about project people. Beside Ashley, swimming in gigantic red jeans and a matching sweatshirt and wearing slip-on gold teeth, was Kevin's girlfriend, Shaniqua Page. She was tossing her blond extensions and glaring. Ashley spoke directly into the project girl's ear to make herself audible above the music.

"Why you gotta scream in my ear?" snapped Shaniqua. "I ain't deaf!"

"*Sorry.* The song's a little loud."

"What song? Ain't no *song* playin'. That's *rap.*"

"Oh. Whatever. I was just saying I'm somewhat out of my *element* here. Are you from this neighborhood too?"

"*Hell* no, I ain't from these punk-ass projects. I'm from the Fort."

"The *Fort?*"

"Sho'nuff! Fort Crest lays 'em and slays 'em, we yokes 'em and smokes 'em!"

Ashley raised her eyes to the ceiling as if making a silent plea.

"Uh-huh. Okay. Well, I'm here with my brother, Jesse, who's with his . . . uh . . . date."

"You mean that girl Raven? They s'pose to be hookin' up, right?"

"Please." Ashley sighed. "Don't remind me. Yes, they're getting married. Anyway, this scene is so new to me. We're not from the area." She was beginning to feel light-headed. She'd skipped dinner, expecting there'd be lots of home-cooked food, which she had looked forward to as a nice change from eating out all the time. But ages had passed and nothing had been brought out.

"Is there going to be something to *eat* later? I'm starved! And this drink is so sweet it *has* to be a diabetes risk. I mean, there's nothing in it but sugar, with some water and purple coloring. It's like drinking grape syrup. Gross." With that, she emptied her Kool-Aid down the drain.

Shaniqua was keeping an eye on her man and hardly listening to this lame girl who put the *stuck* in stuck-up. But when she saw what Ashley had done, she turned her full attention on the student like a high beam of hot, blinding light.

"Why you dump the Kool-Aid out—you sick? Ain't a damn thing wrong with it. I woulda drunk it. Everybody know you gotta let the ice melt to water it down so it ain't too sweet." She frowned at the purple stain in the sink. "What a waste. Here, eat some Cheez Doodles if you so hungry."

Ashley flinched. "No, *merci*, I've been stuffing my face with those stale things all night. Isn't there anything *else*?

I don't know," she said, her tone becoming sarcastic, "maybe a potato chip or a pretzel to mix it up a little?"

Shaniqua ignored her and Ashley looked again toward the ceiling. "I'm dead," the college girl murmured under her breath. "I died and went to ghetto hell."

Shaniqua overheard and was *not* having it. "What you talkin' 'bout, Ashy?"

"Ash*ley* . . ."

"You not in no *ghetto*. These the *projects*."

Suddenly Ashley felt nervous. She sure didn't want to get on the wrong side of this homegirl, who seemed awfully dangerous and so easily provoked. "Hey, I really didn't mean to offend, really, Shamika . . ."

"I *told* you my name Sha-*ni*-qua, like Taniqua only with a 'sha,' " she said, pushing up the arm of her sweatshirt to reveal her name tattooed on her shoulder.

"I'm sorry, truly I am . . . Sha-*ni*-qua. Please just ignore anything I say. It's the hunger and fatigue. I'm sure you and your friends are as nice as . . . anyone."

"These bozos ain't my friends. Why you think I'm in this kitchen with you?!"

Ashley noted with annoyance that Shaniqua said "you" as if she were describing the last wretch on the planet. Her eyes quickly scanned the crowd. Where was Jesse?

"Take Miss Ice Capades over there," Shaniqua continued, gesturing toward Aisha, who'd removed her skates and was leaning against Max. "I don't care *how* much bank she get off them tired TV commercials, she still wak, clunkin' around on four wheels when everybody else rockin' blades! She can't stand me because I took her man Kev. The cute one with the Knicks cap. Over by the window, see him? *We* together now. So that's what *that's* about. Ain't no friends of mine up in here, and that's word. Me and the rest of these hoes, we like grease and water."

"Oil and water," Ashley mumbled. Then she said out loud, "I see what you mean, absolutely, and am so down with you on that." She felt she'd taken enough abuse from this ruffian, who probably didn't even have her GED. "Well, better go check on my little brother. Nice meeting you."

Shaniqua looked Jesse's sister up and down without answering. She took a handful of Cheez Doodles and pushed them into her mouth. A light dusting of orange powder was left clinging to her chin.

Ashley squeezed through the crowded hallway and pushed her way into the jammed living room, fleeing Shaniqua as much as seeking Jesse.

2

*T*he party was settling into a lower gear and people had found seats on everything from speakers to sofa arms. Keeba made her way to the table, covered now with empty platters. "Where the Cheez Doodles go?!" she yelled to nobody in particular. "And y'all greedies guzzled down the last drop of Kool-Aid!" She ran her finger over a platter and licked off the powdered cheddar. An Usher song was playing, one of those yearning grooves that make everybody feel like they're in love, even people—like Keeba—who didn't have anyone.

Couples who came to the party together sat close on the couch. Single girls found boys who would do, at least for the moment, and paired off with them in slow dances. Watching, Keeba turned her thoughts from food to romance. She wanted a boyfriend, a real one, not the players blasting Fabolous out their mamas' windows and talking trash about girls and how they like to hit it quick and split. All that because deep down they were scared to be close to a girl. Keeba wanted somebody like Usher, singing now, the kind of guy who fell in love and hung out with you on the phone, who wasn't scared to put his heart into a girl. The fact that Usher was an R&B superstar with a carefully crafted romantic image didn't factor into Keeba's ardor. She knew there was a real-life Usher for her somewhere in Brooklyn. There had to be.

"And what you thinking about so hard?" asked Aisha, noticing her friend staring into space.

Keeba shook off her thoughts and patted Aisha's rounded hair.

"I was wondering if that Afro bite."

Aisha couldn't have agreed more. "Ain't this hair a trip?! They got me looking like Michael Jackson before he got his white-girl hairdo. As soon as this wak sixties retro commercial's done, I'm losing these naps, and fast. If I was still in braids I'd come to you, but now I get my hair done in Midtown."

"G'head, be all that. One day you gon' be begging me to put my healing touch on them naps." Keeba rubbed her stomach. "Where all the food go? I'm *hooon*gry."

Aisha put her finger to her lips. "You shoulda said something! I got just what you need." She took Keeba by the arm and led her down the hallway. "Shhh . . ."

"You know I'm not into that, so don't even play."

"Don't be so drama, Kee. You want food, right? Then come on."

Light shone from under the closed bathroom door, which Aisha, without even pausing, pushed open.

Keeba tugged at Aisha's elbow. "Ai! Somebody's in there. What you doing?!"

Aisha shut the door behind them as quickly as she'd opened it. Inside, it took a moment for Keeba's eyes to adjust to the light. When they did, she howled.

"Y'all is . . . is . . . ." She could barely catch her breath. "Sick! And greedy!"

Max and Raven were sitting on the side of the bathtub. Toya was in the bathtub with a pillow at her back. Ashley was next to Jesse on the floor, her back resting against the toilet bowl. A towel was spread out on the floor as if this were a Prospect Park picnic. Empty White Castle hamburger boxes, ketchup-stained french-fry bags, packs of onion rings, and soda cans were all scattered about. The diners were grinning. Ashley lifted the bag next to her.

"Help yourself," she said through a mouthful of food.

Aisha slid in between Max and Raven.

"The party's kicking and all," Aisha said, "but, Kee, y'all gots to *feed* folks, especially dancing folks. Max had to drive way out on Atlantic Avenue to save us from starvation!"

"I gotta go get my sister!" Kee said.

Back in the living room, Keeba found Teesha and whispered in her ear.

Shaniqua was watching the sisters as they giggled and hurried down the hall. She followed. When they ducked into the bathroom and closed the door, Shaniqua nodded to herself, thinking, So *that's* where everybody went! They was in the bathroom *smokin'*! Well, she damn well wasn't gonna be left out. Maybe she'd start having a good time. Kevin wasn't paying her no attention no way, so she might as well join the *real* party. She pushed open the door without knocking. "Yo, I'm down, too. What y'all got?" Her eyes met Aisha's and for a moment they stared at each other like boxers at a weigh-in.

Teesha held up a bag. "Hamburgers."

"Hamburgers?" said Shaniqua in disgust. "I thought y'all had something for the *head*. Nobody want no damn *burgers*."

Aisha couldn't resist a good diss of her old enemy. "From the looks of that chin, I see you already had plenty to eat."

Shaniqua's chin was still tinted Cheez Doodle orange.

Max nudged Aisha with his elbow. "Chill, Ai."

Jesse giggled. Ashley laughed out loud. Teesha and Keeba snickered. Toya smiled and shook her head. Raven held her breath.

Shaniqua wiped her chin real fast. "Don't tess me, roller girl, 'cause I will roll your behind right out this window!"

Aisha jumped to her feet. "Don't tess *me*, girlfriend, 'cause I *will* pass it with a straight A and beat the blond off you."

"Oh will you? You and what crew? 'Cause you can't take me by yourself. Maybe your man can help you out." She ran her eyes over Max. "Yeah, I wouldn't mind a little pro wrestling with *him*. I already took one man from you, and I can do it again."

Goosebumps spread across Aisha's body like she'd stepped from a heated room into winter. Beads of sweat collected at her temples. Her nostrils flared. Then the former street brawler did something uncharacteristic. She took a deep breath, counted to ten inside, and asked herself if it was really worth it to beat down this scrub. She had a good job, Max, and her two great children, Starlett and Ty. Blondie had nothing. So what if Shaniqua had gotten Kevin to creep her way while he was still supposed to be Aisha's man? He wasn't about nothing no way, never even showed interest in the kids he'd brought into the world. Now those kids called Max "Daddy." No, Blondie wasn't worth standing up over. Aisha sat down.

"You hear that, Max? She got hopes for *you*, now that I let her have my other *leftovers*. Here, Blondie, have this too," she said, holding out a half-eaten hamburger.

Shaniqua smacked the hamburger onto the floor and stormed off, leaving the door wide open. A few minutes later there was a loud crash. Teesha and Keeba went tearing from the bathroom, followed by the others, and found Shaniqua standing over a splatter of broken glass.

"Oops. My elbow musta hit it by mistake," she said nonchalantly.

Keeba stared at the shards of aqua blue glass for a moment before she realized that she was looking at what had been her mother's brand-new-should-still-be-in-the-box punch bowl. The one they weren't supposed to touch. She flung herself at Shaniqua.

"You little . . . !"

They slammed into the table and fell to the floor. In an instant, Teesha was on her too. It took the combined strength of Max, Jesse, and Kevin to haul the sisters, punching and kicking, off the flailing girl.

"Make that fiend pay for it!" someone shouted.

"Yank them gold teef out and pawn 'em!" said someone else.

Before any reimbursement could be had, Kevin was bustling his enraged girlfriend out the door. "Payback's a bitch, bitches!" Shaniqua screamed over her shoulder.

A good fight is sometimes just the energy boost a waning party needs, and soon the dance floor was packed again with teenagers whooping and rocking. Eventually, though, with nothing left to eat or drink and hours of dancing weighing down their legs, people began leaving. It was well past midnight when Keeba and Teesha turned the lock, slid on the chain to their apartment door, and dropped fully dressed onto their beds.

Morning came through the window, lighting up bodies lying this way and that in the living room. Most everybody had gone home, but a few kids had passed out where they sat. Their hostesses, still sleepy but bent on cleaning up before their mother's return, invited the stragglers to leave also.

"Git up!" ordered Keeba, flicking on the blinding white halogen lamp. "Git out!"

A girl curled in the corner behind the stereo raised her head. A long zipper mark from the jacket she'd folded into a pillow was imprinted on her cheek like a train track. Her hair was smushed in on one side and sticking straight out on the other.

"Hit it, Frankenstein," yelled Keeba in the girl's face. "The party's over!"

The girl was squinting and blinking. "Where breakfast?"

Keeba called to Teesha, who was cleaning up the kitchen, "Tee, Cynthia here wanna know where breakfast at!"

"What?! Tell her up the block on the corner. The store opens at eight."

Cynthia's head dropped back down. "That's not right."

Deciding to ignore her dozing guests, Keeba turned on BET's *Video Soul Countdown*. After kicking the vacuum cleaner a couple of times, she got it working. Its motor coughed, sputtered, and suddenly blared into a roaring staccato that sounded like gunfire. She sang and jerked her shoulders to the sultry rhythms of Ashanti's latest single, vacuuming around bodies. Moans and groans came from different corners of the living room as the last party-goers dragged themselves to their knees, balanced on sore feet, and stumbled out the door and toward the elevator.

"Tee! Usher's on! Hurry up!"

Keeba huddled close to the TV screen as if doing so meant she could be seen by the singer. Teesha came running, soapy water dripping from her hands. The singer with the sweet face and rippled stomach bounced and grinned, doing his own dance, the U-turn. The sisters, imitating his every move, bounced and grinned too.

And out at the Newark Holy Tabernacle of the Pentecost, Sister Edwina Percy Washington bounced and grinned as well, banging her tambourine to the last gospel song before the bus ride home.

3

Summertime was sizzling and the outdoor benches were in hot demand. Older women dominated the front benches like gatekeepers on watch. Neighbors for decades, they knew the private lives of most everyone who happened by. Like the girl who wasn't showing yet but was pregnant, the man who drank up his check every payday, the lady who was hospitalized because of "sugar," the teenage boy the cops were looking for—the projects had no secrets from these sleuths. And when the women didn't actually know things, like tabloid journalists they made them up.

"Umm-hmm, as I live and breathe I know that for a *fact*. She chased the girl buck naked 'round the hallway, then went back in the apartment and took a mop handle to her no-good husband. Beat the devil right out of him, yes she did."

"You know Miss Frost down on three? Yes, you *do* know Miss Frost—she big and tall and hunch over when she walk! Her grandchild got one of them harelips, poor thing, was almost cute. Well, she hit the number *big* last week but don't want nobody to know."

"Well, *I* heard that the Koreans who just moved in on the first floor is collecting welfare. And they own half them Korean salad places in Manhattan, yes they do!"

On the opposite side of the building, children chased each other over and under the back benches, which they ruled. They played as parents kept an eye on them from windows high above the checker tables and box-ball squares. Life had taught these children a few simple lessons in their short years. Grass was better ripped from the ground and thrown in someone's hair than just growing. Hard candy was better chewed than sucked no matter how bad it made their teeth ache. And all thoughts were better hollered than quietly said.

The benches at the side of the building were shrouded in the shadows of massive trees bearing initials cut into the wide trunks. This was where young people with little to do hung out, joking, dissing, and arguing about everything from the best basketball team to the worst J. Lo video. The topic of the moment was the future of the projects, and the talk was getting heated.

Teesha shoved the palm of her hand an inch from

Arkim's nose, making the young man's muscular pit bull, Homey, stir protectively.

"Talk to the hand! Talk to the hand!" Tee snapped, turning the back of her head to Arkim. "The face be busy."

Arkim pushed away her hand. "Why you gotta give attitude? I'm only telling you what my old man said, that the projects probably be going co-op in a couple of years, and whoever don't have mad cash gonna be out on the street. Don't be getting mad at *me* over it—I'm just the messenger. Whites taking over all them buildings by the East River, and when there ain't no more room for them down there, they coming this way."

Tee rolled her eyes. She had heard the rumors too, and they worried her. It seemed like everything in life depended on money, something she had too little of. Her mother's monthly check was already stretched to the max, and Mrs. Washington wouldn't be able to get by at all if Teesha and Keeba didn't help her out with their hair-braiding money. How were they supposed to be able to buy a co-op, even if it was their own dumpy project apartment?

"You'd believe anything, Arkvark. That's why you're headed right back to the eleventh grade. The Jackson 5 getting back together too, right? And Venus and Serena giving up tennis for golf. Oh yeah, O.J. didn't kill them two people either." She paused for breath. "White people are not moving into no run-down housing project. Besides, where would they put *us*? Why you think they built

Brooklyn Heights? So white people wouldn't have to live with us in these broke-down, broke-elevator, broke-people projects."

But Arkim wouldn't back down. "You know Housing would fix everything up first, make it a real co-op for rich people."

"Right, son. Rich people living up in here with *you*. I don't *think* so," said Teesha.

Most of the time Keeba was down with whatever her sister said, but she was with Arkim on this one. "But that's what happened near where Raven's boyfriend Jesse live. Raven said white folks moved to the neighborhood and made everybody's rent go up. I think Arkim's right, Tee, that's how gentrofaction work."

Arkim winked and nodded his head in agreement.

"You get mad *duh*s for that, Kee," said Teesha. "Jesse's folks got enough bank to own their house, so they don't even pay rent. Anyway, the projects under rent control, so our rent can't go up but so much. Besides, you have to *buy* a co-op, and that means big up-front cash. And, *duh-head*, the word's 'gentrification.' You and Arkim—both y'all belong on the same retard ward."

"Whatever," Keeba answered, like she wasn't bothered.

Arkim wanted to say something in Keeba's defense but figured why waste breath. Tee was always ready with a diss, like she memorized them. It wasn't that he didn't like Tee—he thought both the sisters were cool—but she was steady cutting people down, like the comics on BET who always found the one audience member with a dry-looking weave. Keeba, though, could be funny without making you feel bad. Plus he could tell she liked him even if she tried to play it off like she didn't.

A young woman with short natural hair was heading their way, bouncing on her toes as she walked. A cloth bag marked "Brooklyn Public Library," heavy with books, swung from her shoulder.

Keeba waved, eager to turn the attention to someone else. "Hi! Girl, you gonna break your shoulder off lugging that big bag around. How's the liberry?"

The woman set her bag down on the bench. "The li-*brary* is still there and waiting for you guys to join. You don't have to pay, you know. It's free. We ask only that you read."

As strange as a fish swimming *down*stream to spawn, Skye March had moved from her middle-class condo to the projects. Her friends thought she'd gone crazy. But the librarian was on a mission. Inner-city teens, she said, didn't benefit from occasional school visits by condescending professionals the kids never saw again. They needed to witness success, to have role models living among them.

"Wassup, Skye? Oh, *you* up because you the sky. Ha, ha." Arkim repeated the same joke every time he saw her. "Hey, you got a dollar I can borrow? Me and Homey thirsty."

"No, I don't have a dollar you can borrow, Arkim." Skye

had gotten used to the kids hitting her up for money ever since the one time, when she was still new to the neighborhood, she had lent someone on her floor five dollars for Pampers and baby food, only to find out later that the girl had no children. Word had gone out that Skye was an easy touch. "I'm sure the water faucets in your apartment are working fine if you're that thirsty. How are you otherwise?"

"I'm cool, just kickin' it with these two honeys, who're dissin' me as usual."

"Pray tell, why are you two dissing such a nice guy?"

Teesha and Keeba exchanged glances. *Pray tell. Dissing.* Skye was nice, but the way she talked was corny.

Prompted by her sister's putdown, Keeba switched sides. She said, "Arkim so wak, he think Elvis alive."

Arkim punched her in the side.

"And he's so ignorant," added Teesha, "he said O.J.'s innocent."

Skye sat down next to her bag of books.

"I'm sorry to say so, but Presley's resurrection and Simpson's innocence are about as equally likely. As African Americans we're all too willing to find the noble victim in some sick guy in a jealous rage who . . . Don't get me started on this one Arkim, look at the evidence and . . ."

Teesha nudged her sister, chuckling.

"I ain't even said what they said I said!" interrupted Arkim. "Everybody know the deal with O.J., I ain't that stupid. They playin' you. What I was saying is that whites getting ready to buy up the projects and throw us out."

"Oh that." Skye had been doing a lot of hand-holding over the past few months on that very subject. Some of the elders had heard the rumor too and had panicked, afraid they'd have nowhere to go. Skye was certain the city would never do anything that politically risky. "Arkim, no group is gearing up to invade Hillbrook Houses."

Teesha sneered at Arkim. "That's what I'm trying to tell this weakest link. Them people don't want a thing to do with us."

"Teesha," Skye said, turning to her, "there's no such thing as 'them people,' grammatically or actually. You know how certain people lump all of *us* in with every African American and refer to us as 'those people,' whereas in reality we're all different, with various viewpoints and attitudes? That's exactly what you're doing."

Teesha leaned back and yawned. Arkim scratched the hairs sprouting on his chin. Humming, Keeba picked at slivers of wood sticking up from the bench slats.

The librarian went on, "It's true, a good number of young professionals and artsy types with bucks have bought lofts in the empty factories a few blocks from here. And yes, most of them are white, but some are Asian and a few are African American. It's because rents are so high in Manhattan that people are looking to the other boroughs for affordable housing. But public housing is owned by the City of New York and no one, of any color, can just sweep in and buy these complexes out from under us. The projects are not, and cannot be, for sale. End of story."

"I told you," jeered Teesha. "Duh!"

"Yeah," added Keeba. "Duh."

Just then Butta appeared, bouncing a basketball. Pushing fifty, he was the classic old-school project man, still in sneakers and sweats, still perfecting his jump shot. Born in Hillbrook, he worked as a handyman for the Housing Authority.

"Wassup with the Bench Generation? Oh, I don't mean you, my sister of the library." He winked at Skye. "When y'all gettin' jobs?"

"When you learn how to dunk," answered Arkim.

Butta dribbled, faked a pass, and went up for an air dunk. "How ya like me now, son? Maybe one day you be ready to hit the court with the big dawg."

Arkim shrugged, not impressed.

Skye, however, was impressed, but not by the man's basketball skills. Butta was quite muscular and in excellent shape for someone his age. For someone any age, actually. But she kept her distance. He was simply too project, a grown man dressed like a teenager—really. And what kind of name was "Butter"? Certainly not that of an adult role model.

"Hi, Butter. We were discussing reverse white flight. Folks here are beginning to worry that white people might be coming back." She was curious to know what this Peter Pan of the projects thought.

"What, y'all mean the new settlers frontin' down in Waterfront? They spell nothin' but trouble for the People's

Republic of the Projects. If ya don't know it now, now ya know it."

He dribbled the ball fast between his legs, then got it spinning on his finger, slapping it over and over to keep it going. "Back in the *day*, Eldridge and Bobby and Huey told the people what time it was. Nowadays, the Bench Generation ain't up on the struggle to break the chains of—"

Skye touched the spinning basketball, sending it whirling to the ground.

"Hey, don't mess with a brother's game! You lookin' at the next NBA-draft free agent."

"Right," said Skye, "and you're looking at the next Condoleezza. I just didn't want that swirling orb to hypnotize you back to the sixties. You might not find your way out to reality."

"Whoa, diss! She dissin' me, right y'all?" He dribbled, spun around, and did an air layup. "Two points! That's ahight 'cause Butta smooth as butter and got the jump shot to go widdit. The sixties *is* reality, Miss Brooklyn Public. The *now* is madness. See, y'all members of the Bench Bunch ain't up on the insanity. You up *in* it, but you ain't up *on* it. Y'all warring over the blues and reds instead of fightin' for the *black*."

Skye understood what Butta was saying. She felt terribly troubled by what she was seeing around the neighborhood. Project kids were falling into the trap of gang life, and were maiming and even killing each other over colors and turf. She was particularly disturbed that girls were joining gangs in increasing numbers and that, like the boys, they were ending up disfigured, behind bars, or both. If only she could get young people to see other, better ways to live, if only they'd come to the library . . .

"Butter's absolutely right on this one," Skye said. "Kids think the gang's about family, but no family would let its members kill or be killed over a red jersey or a blue cap. That's plain sick."

On this point the bench fell into unanimous agreement.

Keeba remembered a newspaper article that said girls had to beat up a stranger to get in a gang. Teesha had heard that a teacher at Franklin High was punched out cold when she tried to make a girl take off her red bandanna. Arkim's uncle had been shot for wearing a blue sweatshirt in the wrong part of Brooklyn.

"When I was a young brother," said Butta, "everybody was down with the same colors, the red, black, and green of the black liberation flag. This madness y'all talkin' about is jacked up." He paused for a moment and then challenged Arkim. "So you got game, Holmes, you can dunk? Then bring it on—the courts at Shady Rest are waiting."

Arkim accepted with a smirk, and the girls watched as he and Butta headed up the hill, dribbling and passing the basketball back and forth while Homey scampered from one man to the other.

When she first moved to the projects Skye was stunned to discover how few kids had any direction or goals. Forget a five-year plan, these teens didn't even have a five-day forecast. She had taken it upon herself to try to reach out to as many as possible. Now, as Butta and Arkim made their way to the basketball court, she posed her usual question to the two brand-new high school graduates.

"Future plans? I don't know if I got a future," responded Keeba.

"Getting paid" was Teesha's answer. When was *she* ever going to get some real money? None of the good jobs took someone who only had a high school diploma, but Tee wasn't the college type like Raven. And though Aisha, the high school dropout, was getting more bank than all of them, her lucky break in becoming a star in commercials wasn't something that happened to just anyone.

"I guess that's a start, Teesha. You want *something* at least, although money is only a means, not an end in itself. But we'll start there if you like. What can you do to get money? What skills do you have now that you can build on?"

"None."

How many times had Skye heard that answer?

"Everybody has a skill, Teesha. Everybody knows how to do at least one thing well. What do you enjoy?"

"Skating." Teesha slid her feet back and forth.

"Food," Keeba chimed in, inhaling hard and making her stomach stick out.

"Okay, let's look at those things," said Skye, sounding like a teacher. "Teesha, you like to skate, and Keeba, you like to eat. Do those skills tie into any jobs you can think of?"

"Yep," said Keeba, "being one of them skating waitresses."

The girls, each other's best audience as usual, laughed loudly.

"Seriously, guys. You don't want to spend the rest of your life as one of Butter's Bench Generation, do you?"

Teesha waved her hand the way she'd shoo away a fly. "Oh please. Butta's the Hoop Dream Generation, and we on the bench. What's the difference?"

"Butter's employed, for one thing."

Teesha saw little difference in their prospects. "But he's a grown man and still lives at home."

Skye was used to hearing that kind of fatalism, which always sounded as if the kids wouldn't dare to hope for anything, from fear of disappointment. She watched as Keeba absently twisted one of her braids.

"What about hair? Lots of girls are wearing the Washingtons' braids. Did you two ever think about going into business?"

"But we in business already," Teesha said. "We been doing hair since we had dimples on our hands."

Keeba explained, "That's how we get our spending money and help Moms out with the bills." She felt proud of how she could do hair. Maybe she wasn't as quick with the clever lip as Teesha, but when it came down to twisting hair into tight, even, pretty braids, she was damn good.

Skye clapped her hands together. "Then do *that*. You already have the skills and the experience. Grow your client base. Rent out a storefront somewhere. Hire people to work for you. Why not? Hair has always been a business opportunity in our communities. Like funeral parlors."

"And where all this cash for rent and paychecks supposed to come from?" asked practical-minded Teesha.

"Where all capital for business comes from, be it Johnson & Johnson or the neighborhood dry cleaners—investors. Talk to people who might have extra money."

"I don't know where in the sky you come from," said

Teesha, "but in these projects, money don't come in 'extra.'"

"Teesha, you have to have faith in the people around you. You might be surprised. How does that Michael Jackson song go? 'You are not alone.'"

Teesha sucked her teeth. "Michael Jackson's not alone because he got all them little monkeys and baby pigs for company. And as tight as he is with his cash, he should be singing 'You can't get no loan.'"

The girls burst out laughing again. Once they'd composed themselves, Keeba stood and stretched. "All this talk make my knees ache."

"I best be getting upstairs anyway," Skye said, picking up her bag. "Got a new batch of books to review. Nice kicking it with you guys. And remember, if you don't want to go all the way to the library, you know where I live. I have lots of good books. And think about what I said."

"Nice kicking wi*choo*, Miss March," said Keeba, smiling slyly at her sister, who chuckled. "We going around to the front to yoke old ladies for they cash so we can get this hair thing started, right, Tee?"

"Right you be. Holla at ya later, Skye."

"Okay, you girls be good." The librarian headed up the block, bouncing on her toes. As soon as she was out of sight, Keeba started walking in circles, imitating Skye.

Teesha giggled. "You know you need to stop. That ain't right—Skye our girl. She just different."

"Oh yes, dear. Me and Miss Liberry always be chill*ing*

and kick*ing* 'cause our love is *king*! *Dring, dring."* Keeba bounced all the way to the front of the building, holding her pinky in the air and swishing her hips.

Mrs. Washington was settled at the end of the bench, fanning her face with her hand. A row of women in colorful plaids and prints perched alongside her like birds on a ledge. She felt someone behind her and looked quickly over her shoulder.

"Gimme that bag!" yelled Keeba as she snatched her mother's large pocketbook with the broken zipper.

"Oh!" Mrs. Washington cried, truly startled for a second. "Keeba!"

Keeba ran across the street toward the jingling sounds of the ice-cream truck, pressing the pocketbook tight to her chest.

"Teesha! Go get that fool sister of yours! Darting out in the street like that, not even looking where she's going! Child crazy as a betseybug!"

Teesha raced after Keeba. The other women laughed and slapped their thighs.

"Good thing I hid my wallet with my ID, checks, and little bit of money deep in the lining, safe from pickpockets. She won't find even a wooden nickel in that big ol' bag. That'll show her."

"Those two of yours are something *else* again!" said one woman.

"Neither one looking a day older than ten," added another. "Seems like yesterday they were so little and cute in their stroller like two peas in a pod."

"And they sure can braid some hair," said a third. "I like how the young people be wearing them twisses. When they gonna do yours, Sister Washington?" she asked, cutting her eyes at Mrs. Washington's thick nappy hair gathered into a strained bun.

Mrs. Washington had things other than hair on her mind. "See how them girls are? I sent that other one after my bag, now they're *both* over there getting into heaven knows what with *my* pocketbook. If their father was here . . ." Mr. Washington had passed away when Teesha and Keeba were still little. Heart attack right there in his office at Sanitation, where he'd made supervisor. The pension he left was just enough for them to get by on.

Keeba stepped into view from the side of the ice-cream truck. Her mother's pocketbook hung from her shoulder. She was grasping a double cone with two mountainous swirls of strawberry ice cream under a blanket of sprinkles. And she was smiling, licking pink drips from her knuckles. The rowdy laughter from the bench turned into coughing, then back to laughter.

"Hmph, Sister Washington, it sure is a good thing you hid that wallet!"

"If you ask me, it look like she found a lot more than your wooden nickel. How much you all think them double cones go for, a dollar fifty?"

"No, ma'am, they asking that much for a plain old regular cone! I remember when children would go chasing after the ice-cream man with quarters in they little hands and come back with all kinds of Popsicles and cones. Nowadays, you gotta hit the number to afford anything off the truck."

Then Teesha appeared at her sister's side, sipping a large chocolate milkshake through a straw, a mound of whipped cream floating on top. The traffic light turned green and red and green again. Neither girl made a move to cross the street. Together they posed in the bright sun, licking and sipping, flashing big smiles at the bench.

Mrs. Washington watched them, shaking her head. She couldn't help but chuckle, despite herself. They were so silly. "Umm-hmm, that's all right," she said in a threatening tone. "I'll get them."

The others looked from Mrs. Washington to her daughters and back again, elbowing one another and giggling. The WALK sign came on several times before Keeba finally pushed the last bit of soggy cone in her mouth and Teesha made a noise like a sink emptying as she sucked up the last of the bubbly brown foam through her straw. They wiped their mouths with their hands and darted through the traffic, expertly dodging oncoming cars.

"Here ya go, Ma," said Teesha. "I got your bag back from this purse snatcher. You want something from the truck?"

Keeba gave her mother a loud smack of a kiss on her cheek. "Yummm . . . Thank you *sooo* much."

Mrs. Washington tilted her head up and raised her eyebrows, meaning she was not *even* bothered by their foolishness. "I'll give you both 'Thank you.' If there's even so much as a penny missing . . ." She opened the pocketbook and fumbled around inside it, feeling for her wallet. The women, buzzing with anticipation, cheerfully described what *they'd* do if *their* children pulled a stunt like that.

"I'd get me a switch off one of these trees and I don't care how old they are, I'd let 'em have it!"

"A leather strap, nice and worn, would work just fine for me!"

"You ladies remember them flyswatters our folks used on us?"

A smile spread across Mrs. Washington's face as her hand touched the familiar lumpy square, exactly where she'd tucked it.

"I knew they were bluffing, trying to pull the wool over my eyes," she exclaimed. She grabbed at Keeba's arm but the girl leaped out of reach. "You just wait till I get you upstairs, tormenting your old mother. And that goes for you too, Teesha!"

5

*R*aven flinched in pain. "Ouch! Hellooo . . . There's skin under that hair you're yanking on!" She held up the hand mirror so she could see the back of her head reflected in the large mirror behind her.

Teesha's fingers were flying, folding sections of hair over each other and scooping up more as she worked the thick hair into a skinny braid, neat and tight to Raven's head.

"The price of beauty runs high, Rave. That's what my mother said whenever she raked through my peasy hair. I was real tender-headed when I was growing up and I'd scream while the peas popped. Now turn your head this way before I have to clunk you with this comb like Edwina used to do me."

Raven dared Teesha to even *think* about hitting her with that comb. "Just because I'm in college doesn't mean I won't beat you right down to the ground. And another thing, I'm *sooo* sick of that same tired 'tender head' story you tell every time you do my hair."

Teesha ignored the threats and complaints and kept braiding. Summer made her feel happy for a lot of reasons—warm weather, fast skates, Italian ices—but mostly because Raven was home, which made it feel like the good old days when they were in high school. Those were fun times. Sitting behind goody-two-shoes Toya and teasing her with jokes until she turned red before busting out loud. Lunchtime in the cafeteria with the Hillbrook girls—Keeba, Raven, Aisha, and Toya—taking over a table and being so loud the attendants were constantly on their case. Food fights, bombing Aisha with bread rolls and fruit over some nonsense about boys.

It was all good then, before Aisha decided to drop out for the hell of it and later started having babies. Before Raven got pregnant her senior year and had to drop out. Before Toya discovered computers and got all serious. Teesha didn't talk about it, but she had fantasized about going to college herself. She thought she was pretty smart, but the only good grades she ever got were in math. The other subjects bored her and she flunked them, which got her left back. Something she felt really ashamed of. Dropping out was cooler because it was something you did on purpose. Being left back a grade meant you had tried—and failed. At least it hadn't happened twice to her, like it did to Keeba. But still . . .

This put her in awe of Raven, the only one of their group to make it to college. And it made her disappointed in herself, but those were feelings she kept quiet about. She and Keeba had wondered if Raven would change, act different, since she was so far from the projects at a fancy school. But Raven was still her girl, still one of the girls. Mostly.

"Ow! All right, that's it, let me out of this chair! I'm going downstairs to Toya." Raven was rubbing her hairline at the neck.

"Come on, Rave, chill! I'm sorry—I was daydreaming and pulled too hard. Don't get up. My mind slipped. Toya isn't doing hair these days anyway. She's in computer class all day and studies all night. So you stuck with me, unless you want to go out in the street looking like Macy Gray on one side of your head and Alicia Keys on the other."

"Tee, I'm not playing with you. If you hurt me one more time, I am so out of here. Where's Kee? I want *her* to do my braids."

"*I am so out of here. I am so out of here.* Where you get *that*? From one of your Susie Cornfield college friends?"

"From ya mama. Where's Kee!"

"Kee hurts worse than me. She's hanging outside somewhere, probably at the card table in the back. Would you simmah down nah! You get *Saturday Night Live* at your school? You know the 'simmah down nah' lady? She is *sick* she so funny."

"Never seen it. I don't even know what you're saying."

"Simmer . . . down . . . now. See, she works at the return desk in this store and soon as somebody walks up . . . Oh, never mind. So tell me, what's school like up there in farm country? You have a good GPO or GPA or whatever it is?"

"My grades are decent. And I'm only an hour upstate from the city, no farms anywhere around, we're basically in the 'burbs. All I can tell you, girl, is once you start moving in a certain direction, away from the projects, you have one hurdle after another—first, getting admitted, then dealing with *real* different people, then fighting to maintain good grades to keep your scholarship, then learning how to interview and job-hunt. And I still have to be a good fiancée to Jesse and a great long-distance mom to Smokey, who drives his grandmother crazy. That's what it's like, Tee. But I'm hanging." She sighed and slumped against the chair.

"And I thought you were having fun, being a party coed." Tee studied the row of braids. "Leave the back loose?"

"Yeah, so it hangs down. Don't think I'm complaining, though. College is what I wanted. And when I think of the alternative, that makes me want it even more. I wasn't cut out to stay a project girl my *whole* life."

Teesha whacked Raven's head with the comb. "And what's so bad about being a project girl, Miss Thang?!"

Raven sniggled. "Simmer down now!"

Teesha pulled her ear.

"All right, all right. Can't take a joke? Anyway, I didn't say *anything* was wrong with *being* a project girl. We'll always be that. But do you want to *live* like one forever, stuck in these tiny apartments, praying the elevator works, hoping no thug's waiting for you on the staircase, wishing to win Lotto? What *are* you and Kee going to do now anyway, look for jobs? Go back to school? College is right for some people, but it's not for everybody. There are other ways to make it besides academics."

It was Teesha's turn to sigh. "I kinda thought about college, but with my grades . . ." She changed the subject to Skye's idea about her and Keeba opening a hair salon, hiring people to work for them, having lots of clients, and making big money. But she didn't know squat about how to get a plan like that going—finding the place, getting up the rent, making it work. After all, she only had her high school diploma. And she got that a year later than she should have. Raven turned around in the chair, her hair pulling from Teesha's fingers.

"Hey, you graduated from high school. That puts you right on par with Bill Gates from Microsoft, who only has his high school diploma too. He never graduated from college. By now he probably has a hundred honorary degrees, but they don't make him a college man. Tee, half the business execs out there aren't college graduates." Raven felt excited. "That is the perfect idea for you and Kee. You're good, you're known in the neighborhood . . . you can do this, girlfriend!"

The only problem was the same one that always crept up between a project girl and her dreams—money. Still,

Teesha did the financial calculations, Raven figured out the business basics, and together they came up with a plan. Teesha twisted in the rest of Raven's braids while Raven talked about logos and publicity and celebrities with braids.

The Greenwich Village Rap 'n Roll rink was packed with the weekend crowd of college students, Village natives, and party people from all the boroughs. Teesha, Keeba, and Raven walked past the long line snaking around the corner and straight up to the front door. The barrel-chested doorman placed himself directly in their path as if he thought the girls might make a mad dash inside without paying the ten-dollar cover.

"May I help you ladies?"

Raven spoke. "Yes, thanks. We should be on the guest list. Raven Jefferson, Keeba Washington, and Teesha Washington."

His finger traveled down a page. "Jefferson, Jefferson, Jefferson," he mumbled to himself, searching the page. He looked up. "Guests of?"

"Aisha Ingram."

His expression changed for the better. "Ai! Okaaaay, I gotcha." He turned the page to another list. "You ladies aren't on our regular guest list—you're on Ai's personal VIP list. Go right in, ladies, and have a good time."

The Hillbrook girls stuck out their chests and strode in with big smiles. The flash of strobe lights and the thump of music hit them so hard they didn't see Aisha skate over to the edge of the rink.

"Rave, partaaay! Tee! Kee! Hey y'all!" She was waving both arms.

"There she is!" shouted Raven, spotting Aisha standing still as other skaters whizzed by.

"Wassuuup?!" yelled Aisha, waving harder. "Go to the Blade Booth and give them your names! Y'all don't have to pay!"

Soon Raven, Teesha, and Keeba were rolling out onto the smooth, slick surface one after another. Aisha skated toward them, arms wide open, and the group hugged, squealing and shrieking. Jay-Z rapped about "gettin' this money," and Fabolous got the whole house chanting "Holla back, young'n" while they skated around and around inside the enormous rink, passing one another, playing chase, cruising side by side. The crowd seemed to know Aisha and she greeted everybody, waving to this one ("Wassup?!"), giving a thumbs-up to that one ("In the house!"), making a peace sign for another ("And ya *know* dat!").

The rumble of rolling wheels and rhythmic beats thickened the air with sound so solid that the skaters were propelled as if by a mighty wind. Time didn't pass—it stopped.

Eventually, the friends stumbled up the stairs to the VIP lounge, stocked with complimentary beverages and snacks, and collapsed in a heap on the velvet sofas.

"You're getting better, Rave," Aisha said. "You only fell three times."

"These for us?" panted Raven, reaching for a bottle of water.

Keeba's forehead was covered with sweat. "My legs feel like they're still vibrating on them blades! Gimme a juice, Tee. I ain't been on skates for that long in ages. I feel like wheels should be where my feet at."

The girls sat at the tinted window of the private box, chatting, eating, and watching the swarm on the floor below. They were rubbing their feet, all except Aisha, who was used to spending hours on wheels. Teesha said props were due—to herself.

"You better watch out, Ai, you see how good I'm getting on my blades. I might be taking over as the Rap 'n Roll girl."

"Tee, the only blade you ever mastered was a switchblade, with your ghetto self."

"Ooooh, diss" filled the lounge.

"That's all right, talk your mess. But watch your back for the new jack."

"I'ma jack *you*," answered Aisha, throwing half a green Chuckle (her favorite candy) at Teesha.

Teesha's knee deliberately bumped Raven's. It was time to bring up the subject she, Keeba, and Raven had discussed yesterday late into the night. Raven was supposed to talk first because she was Ai's best friend and had more juice, being a college girl. Plus, it was mostly Raven's idea.

"So, Aisha," Raven began, "I wanted to run something by you that we've—that is, the girls and I—were wondering about."

"Yeah," said Teesha.

"Uh-huh," said Keeba.

"What madness y'all up to now? I *told* y'all I can't get no Chippendale boys on skates for Hillbrook Day."

"Nooo," protested Teesha, "nothing like that. That was Keeba's wak idea from the start. She was like 'Oooh, see if Ai can get them strippers with the long hair to skate in our project parade.' "

"Uh-uh, you lie," Keeba said, giggling because she knew *she* was lying. "You *loves* them boys."

Teesha put her foot in Keeba's face. "Yeah, right. That's why you *loves* my feet."

In a second they were wrestling with their legs, trying to get at least a toe in the other's mouth. Raven watched in amusement. They were supposed to be future business-women running their own company?

Aisha loved it and egged them on. "Git her, Tee, don't be played! G'head, Kee, she can't dog you like that!"

Raven loudly cleared her throat. "Maybe we should talk another time?"

The Washingtons sprang up from the sofa, hair every which way, blouse buttons undone, a foot missing a sock.

"Come on, Rave, wait—we ready," pleaded Teesha.

Raven started right in. "So, Ai, we have this great idea for a hair-braiding business that we're sure can work." She went on to explain the idea as she imagined it. Jesse's sister, Ashley, was in business school and could surely help them set up. Her own sister, Dell, was a senior paralegal and could definitely give advice on the legal stuff. And Toya could certainly build the Web site. Teesha and Keeba smiled and nodded as Raven talked. The plan sounded good to them, and all they had to do was braid hair. The only problem with all of Raven's surelys, definitelys, and certainlys was that she hadn't asked any of the people she named if they'd help—but Aisha didn't know that.

Aisha was enthusiastic. "That's phat! We *all* blowin' up. You up in college, Toya's doing her computer thing, and now my other girls starting up they own business! We building a project-girl dynasty! I'll send over more nappy heads than your greasy fingers can tug on. Y'all *go*."

Raven looked from Teesha to Keeba. Teesha looked from Keeba to Raven. Keeba smiled weakly. They sat, quiet as mourners.

"What? Why y'all look like that? What I miss?"

Raven leaned back. Teesha and Keeba moved forward. Keeba spoke. "Me and Tee need a loan. We'll pay you back—you know we good for it. Even though we know you got the *dring, dring* and the *bling, bling*, we never asked you for nothing 'cause folks was crawling out cracks like roaches—long-lost cousins and uncles and kinnygarden teachers, everybody. But this plan Rave and Tee came up with—I just feel like it could give me and Tee a chance to—"

"How much?" asked Aisha, crossing her arms on her chest.

Teesha, who had done the math, took over. "Well, Toya checked it out on the Internet, and the going rate would probably be about four hundred dollars a month to rent a small space. By the time you add in electrical and phone and barber chairs—"

"How much?"

"—and different other stuff, and if we say we're going to give it six months—"

"How much? I ain't asking again."

"Five thousand dollars."

"Five thousand dollars? What I look like?"

"That's rounded off," Raven said quickly. "They could probably make it happen with forty-seven hundred. Remember how we said if one of us got paid we would help the others?"

"Forty-seven hundred? What I look like?"

Nobody said a word or even looked at anyone else. Then Aisha broke out into one of her house-shaking guffaws that used to make the entire cafeteria at Franklin High go into hysterics. "I look *that* cheap?! Y'all my *real* homegirls, I mean, my *hold-me-down* homegirls. I'll give you a loan . . . read my fist . . . *loan* . . . for ten grand. I been ready to help y'all out, but all you ever asked me for was free skates."

6

Mrs. Washington placed sweet potatoes, string beans, and a portion of catfish on each plate. The air had grown cooler with the end of summer, and nothing was better for adjusting to a change of weather, she believed, than a good meal. The girls had been running around for weeks like chickens with their heads cut off and not eating like they should. She set three glasses on the table, opened a large can of Hawaiian Punch, and looked in the china cabinet. Now where'd she stick that pretty blue punch bowl?

"So, Ma, when Miss Henriquez closing her candy store?" asked Teesha, chewing.

"Child, how many times I have to tell you? Don't talk with a mouth full of food."

"Ohhh," said Teesha, adopting an English accent, "I forgaaahht."

Keeba snickered, pouring herself another cup of punch.

"Anybody seen my big punch bowl, the one I got brand new at the church Christmas party?" asked Mrs. Washington. "I know I put it away, calling myself hiding it from you two, but I can't find it for the life of me."

"You look in the *claaahh*set?" asked Tee in her royal accent.

Keeba's shoulders shook.

"Teesha Washington, you stop that foolishness right this second or you can go in that back room and eat by yourself! God is my witness, I don't know how you knucklehead children suppose to open a business when you still acting five years old!"

"All right, all right," said Teesha, nudging Keeba. "We're stone serious about the braid salon—that's why we gotta know when Sister Henriquez clearing out the store so we can get in."

Weeks earlier, Mrs. Washington had announced at the Church of the Open Heart that her daughters were opening a beauty parlor. Pastor Theosim E. Phelps had raised his arms in the air, and "Praise the Lord" resounded through the congregation. Her daughters wanted a little spot not too far from the neighborhood, she had said, so if anybody knew of anything . . . Longtime project resident and church member Nilsa Henriquez had leaped to her feet. The store she'd had for years at 155 York Street was located on the edge of Hillbrook Houses, not that far from the Waterfront area. She told the assembly she'd been praying for somebody to take over her lease because she'd grown too old to be chasing down candy thieves.

Teesha and Keeba had signed an IOU to Aisha in return for a ten-thousand-dollar check, which they smelled, kissed, and shouted over for days before giving to their mother to deposit in her bank account. Now the sisters were eager to add walls, windows, a ceiling, and a floor to their dream.

"The clock's ticking on the interest we gotta pay on the loan," lied Teesha. She thought that might make her mother push Miss Henriquez to move faster.

"I thought Ai said we ain't had to worry about no interest," exclaimed Keeba, surprised by Teesha's announcement.

Teesha kicked her under the table. "Well, we do. Duh."

The "duh" sparked Keeba's memory. "Oh, ah-ight, you right, I forgot."

Mrs. Washington wasn't swayed by their little performance and indeed saw right through it.

"Like I told you both yesterday and the day before and the day before that and every day this week, the Lord grants us all that we need but never before its time."

"Then He betta get a new watch because the time is *now*," mumbled Keeba under her breath.

While her daughters cleaned up the dishes, Mrs. Washington retired to her bedroom and sat down with a creak in the armchair she'd had for decades. She turned on her radio to one of the few stations in New York that played classical music, which she found as soothing as a soft spiritual. Her head against the high-backed wooden chair, she closed her eyes. It sure was something, her little girls making a way for themselves in this hard world. They'd managed to avoid the traps that had caught up so many of their friends—pregnancy, drugs, gangs, crime—and had stuck with their schooling. That alone was a blessing for which she was grateful. And now they might get a business going and right there in Hillbrook. She smiled.

Peas in a pod, people said. Not really. She'd raised them exactly the same, but they'd turned out so different. Even though older, Keeba was like the baby sister, with her naive and innocent ways, hungry for a tender kind of attention. And Teesha was a brooder, just as hungry as Keeba, but for money. Aisha wouldn't have asked them for interest, she knew that. The same way she knew about their little teen parties. But they were good girls, and nowadays you had to let your children live if you wanted to keep them happy. Yes, she'd be sure to hurry Sister Henriquez along. Letting her head droop, Mrs. Washington dozed off to the melodies of Debussy.

"Help! Somebody! Help!" Keeba shouted, sprinting from the salon's back office and colliding with the footstool that held Arkim and his bucket. As Arkim crashed to the floor, the pink paint intended for the walls sloshed across the room. Tied up outside, Homey went wild barking.

Teesha stormed in, waving the box cutter she'd been using

to scrape away paper glued to windows. Toya followed, wielding a metal dustpan. Arkim climbed to his feet, dripping.

"You all right, Kee? What's wrong? Who's here?" Teesha had expected somebody to try to take advantage of them during the move-in, but she hadn't imagined it would happen so soon. There weren't even any cash registers in the place yet.

Panting and jumping up and down, Keeba pointed to the office.

Toya whispered, "They got guns?"

Teesha barged into the half-painted room.

"Nobody's in here," she said.

Toya crept closer to the office entrance, holding up her dustpan as if it would shield her from flying bullets. "What's in there?" she asked.

"Some*body* or some*thing* damn well *betta* be in there. Look what you did," snarled Arkim, his shirtless torso and his jeans splattered pink.

"Keeba," demanded Teesha, "what is going on?"

"I saw a mouse!"

A collective groan rose up, a mixture of scorn and relief, followed by threats.

"Guuurrl, I should kick your . . ." growled Arkim, and threw his paintbrush at Keeba.

Teesha snapped, "I could smack you in that brick head of yours!"

Toya was incredulous. "A mouse? A mouse!"

Keeba was still panting. "I'll clean up out here, but I ain't going back in there. Why y'all act like a mouse ain't nothing? I'm scared of mices." She turned her fear and embarrassment against Homey, who continued to bark. "Would somebody shut that stupid dog up!"

Arkim spun around and faced Keeba, his jeans dark pink and his mood fiery red. "Why don't you shut your own lame self up, Keeba! Look at me!"

They all did. Toya saw the boy who had once sat in front of her at Franklin's weekly school assemblies, his six-foot frame blocking her view. Teesha saw ol' left-back Arkvark, who did *not* call *her* sister lame, as *tired* as he was. Keeba saw her flirtatious upstairs neighbor with the dreamy gray eyes and muscular body. Then, as though their eyes suddenly beheld a single vision, the three of them lost it, laughing uncontrollably.

"I'm sorry," bawled Toya, "but boys not supposed to wear pink!"

"I see you got your gang colors, Arkvark," sputtered Teesha. "Who else in your crew—Barbie?"

"Ahhhh," screamed Keeba, tears of laughter streaming, "you should be in that movie *Pretty in Pink!*"

Arkim kicked at his bucket and sent it rolling across the floor. "Paint ya own damn beauty parlor!" He stomped out, grabbing Homey's leash. The dog abruptly stopped barking, cocked his head to the side, and stared at Arkim.

That evening Keeba went to Arkim's apartment to apologize, but the minute he opened the door she got to laughing again. He tried to stay mad but couldn't, and started grinning. She managed to say she was sorry about knocking him down and everything. But, she added, mices was dangerous. Had he seen that old Michael Jackson movie *Ben*? They talked in the hallway for a while before Keeba headed for the elevator.

"Yo Kee," called Arkim.

"What?"

"Ben was a rat."

"Mouse, rat, whatever. It still bite."

The work crew regrouped the next day. After two weeks of nonstop labor, they had completely cleaned, repainted, and exterminated the space that would house the Washingtons' braid salon.

If only the business side of things had gone as smoothly. Ashley was consumed by "B school" and refused to meet with "those homegirls" who, as she pointedly mentioned to Raven, had thrown "that awful Cheetos party." Nor could Raven persuade Dell to get involved. "I could go to prison for impersonating a lawyer," Dell said. And Miss Henriquez was in such a hurry to retire to Puerto Rico that she left them a scribbled address in Staten Island for rent payments but failed to transfer the lease to their names.

None of this bothered the future businesswomen, though. Paperwork drama, said Teesha. Whatever, said Keeba. The sisters were more concerned with finding barber chairs, wall mirrors, hair supplies, and a sign.

One night shortly before the opening, Teesha lay stretched out on her bed while Keeba sprawled on hers.

"Kee. You awake?"

"Yeah. You?"

"Yeah."

"Wassup?"

As critical as she was sometimes of her big sister, Teesha inevitably turned to her for advice and comfort. Keeba had a way of putting a positive twist on the most wak situation. And the older girl's supportive style made Teesha regret how much she mocked Keeba. Not that Teesha meant the things she said. Words just spurted out like a shook-up soda. When she wanted to look good herself. Or was nervous with worry. Or felt premenstrual and plain mean. She rolled onto her stomach and propped herself up on her elbows.

"I'm stressin' and sweatin'. Suppose our parlor doesn't hit like we want it to and we end up braiding the same old knotheads we been doing all along."

"So? We won't be no worse off. It'll be status quo."

"But it won't," Teesha said. "Things are different now. We have to pay rent, electricity, heat, phone, supplies. At home we never think about the cost of things since we get them for free, like utilities. Add to that, all the other stuff we need, like posters, magazines, and flyers. If Skye hadn't made us free copies at work that woulda been another expense. Our cash is holding up so far, but I don't know, Kee . . . what if we fall on our faces and can't even pay Aisha back? One thing's for sure, our prices definitely have to go up. The girls around here have been paying us fifteen dollars since the beginning of time. It's time for a cost-of-living increase."

She rolled back over and stared at the ceiling.

"You need to chill on all that stress," Keeba said. "That's why people say 'the more money, the more headache.' Money don't get you everything no way, or I'd have a boyfriend by now."

"No you wouldn't, because you're broke as me. Wanna talk about something not getting you everything—boys sure don't get you nothing but drama."

Long ago, the sisters had agreed to disagree on the question of boyfriends. Keeba felt that finding the right cute guy would *make* her life, with or without money. Teesha, seeing so many friends' lives derailed by "night riders" who left them with babies, diseases, or both, was cautious, even skeptical, and believed passionately that cash was the key to a free and happy life.

Keeba flipped over so that she was looking down into her sister's face.

"Usher ain't about drama. He about love."

Teesha sucked her teeth long and loud.

"Spare me, please. The only 'usher' you'll ever get anywhere close to will be ushering people carrying popcorn to their seats at the movies."

They laughed.

"Whatever. On the serious side, it ain't as if Ai gonna send a hit squad out for us if we don't pay her back," Keeba said.

"What really irks me," continued Teesha, "is that there's a whole *army* of playa haters out there wanting to see us fail."

"Truedat."

"Kee, nobody says 'truedat' anymore."

"I do. Truedat. Remember them two girls who had that pact to block Venus and Serena from reaching the top? Where are they now? You don't see them on TV anymore. And the Williams sisters *rule* tennis. They so good, they ain't got nobody to play against but each other. We can't be losing our beauty sleep over no playa haters. The way I see it, if any of our peeps can make it, we can too. And ya *know* dat."

"Nobody says that either."

"Aisha do."

Teesha lay thinking. Kee was right—the haters weren't worth her worry. And if Aisha, Raven, and Toya were successful, why not the Washington sisters? She was grateful to have the kind of sister you could really talk to, and promised herself to stop saying "duh" to her so much.

"You all right, Keeba. G'night."

Keeba didn't answer but smiled in the dark.

The grand opening brought out half the high school, most of the neighborhood merchants, and the entire congregation of the Church of the Open Heart. A new business opening in the projects was rare, and one run by residents themselves, unheard of. Squeezed into the salon—which was decorated with balloons and banners, posters of celebrities, and a signed photo of Aisha—were old-timers, curious neighbors, sharp-eyed pickpockets, and a number of the simply jealous. Teesha was too nervous to talk in public, and Keeba said she wasn't making no "Urkel speech," so the task of addressing the guests fell to Skye March.

Tossing long extensions, Skye began: "When I was kicking it with the Washington sisters this past summer, I was impressed by the clear vision they had for their futures. 'We're in business already,' they said prophetically, as this opening proves. We need more of that spirit in Hillbrook, young women with the insight to recognize their skills and the courage to realize their potential. Teesha Washington, Keeba Washington, we applaud you. And on behalf of myself and the Brooklyn Public Library—to which everyone is invited by the way—I offer you these two library memberships!"

Skye led the clapping. Teesha and Keeba climbed down from the client stools, took the cards, shouted, "Venus and Serena in the house!" and started doing the Bump.

For a moment, Skye looked startled, then she laughed, as did everyone but the haters. "And they dance!" she added. "Next on the agenda, I have a few shout-outs—and please hold your applause till the end. To Aisha Ingram, for her investment in the future of Hillbrook Houses; to Sister Edwina Percy Washington and the Church of the Open Heart, for their generous donation of the desk, chair, and stools; to Gleason's Gym, for the wall-length mirror; to Toya Larson, for the creative Web site; and to Arkim Hamilton, for this lovely paint job that, from what I understand, didn't come without personal sacrifice. Finally, a special thanks goes to a personal friend and wonderful artist, Rae Brock, for her beautiful sign. Thank you!"

Mild applause followed.

"Come on, guys, you can do better than that! Let these folks *feel* you!"

Loud clapping echoed through the salon. "And lest I forget . . . thank you, Keeba, for rocking *my* new braids in the house. And now if you'll all step outside, Rae will unveil the sign!"

A young white woman with full lips and arresting blue eyes tugged on a cord. A tarp dropped to the sidewalk. The group clapped, cheered, and barked their admiration, as if the sign made it all real. On a background of pale browns and yellows was painted the black profile of a woman with flying braids beneath "TeeKee's Tresses" in flowing black lettering. Toya pulled out her digital camera and clicked away.

"Children these days got so much ambition, it's just beautiful . . . ," marveled a white-haired woman leaning on a walker.

"That's what it *be* about," said Butta, palming a basketball, "economics, like Brother Malcolm said, keeping the cash in *our* communities. If ya don't know now, now ya know."

"Pink? They trippin'. Them walls are blinding," whispered a neighbor with braids Keeba had done a couple of weeks earlier.

"They shoulda named that dump *Tacky* Tresses," said Shaniqua, observing the scene from the edge of the crowd. "Ain't nothin' in there but two old stools." Her homegirl, whose bushy rust-colored hair framed her freckled face like a burning halo, nodded. Shaniqua hadn't forgotten the fight at the party. In fact, she still thought about it a lot, and hungered for revenge.

Arkim was positioned at a balloon-adorned turntable he had set up next to the salon. At Skye's signal, he put on headphones and blasted Tweet's hit song. Grown women were wiggling their hips like the sexy singer, chanting, "Oops, oh my." Children picked up pinecones and threw them at each other. Teenagers self-consciously danced the Shake. And Hillbrook Houses' newest entrepreneurs went to work in their own salon on their first clients, the sign artist and their own mother.

While Teesha combed parts into Mrs. Washington's thick hair and joked about the price of beauty, Keeba fumbled with Rae's flaxen locks, so slippery she could hardly grip the hair in her fingers. When the braiding was finished, Mrs. Washington's hair was swept up in a gorgeous braided bun and Rae's fell down her back in skinny braids twisted together and held in place by colorful little rubber bands. Over Keeba's mild protests, the artist insisted on giving her not only the full twenty-five-dollar fee but a five-dollar tip too. Mrs. Washington glanced at Teesha's outstretched, expectant hand and slapped it five.

7

The girls partied late into the warm night. Mrs. Washington stayed up waiting, which she rarely did. But this night was special. She was proud of her daughters and, to tell the truth, somewhat surprised. One day, they're giggling and spitting at the table, flashing chewed food in their mouths, and the next they're managing a beauty parlor. God's ways, she thought, are truly mysterious.

When the girls came bustling in, she was there to give each of them a big hug and lead them in a prayer of thanks. In their room, Teesha pulled crumpled bills from her bra and counted the money they'd made in one day. Six paying heads at $25 a shot came to $150—and that didn't even include $18.75 in tips. She added and multiplied imaginary income for a long time until she drifted off into dreams about clothes, concerts, and trips to the

Bahamas. Keeba was dreaming too, but with wide-open eyes. Her dream had happened that afternoon at the opening . . .

Arkim was about to take a break. Aisha's friend Dee Jekyll from the HipHopGame crew was taking over for him.

"Yo, Jekyll," Arkim said, "don't be spinnin' no Nelly or Diddy. They for the MTV set."

Keeba had been keeping an eye on Arkim, despite being cornered by Skye, and was hoping to hang with him. He had impressed her the day she dropped by to apologize about the paint spill. They'd never really talked before then, just mostly joked and dissed each other. So what a surprise to discover he was shy. And nice. He had even said he was sorry for yelling at her, seeing it was only an accident.

Skye was in the middle of trying to convince Keeba that it *did* make a difference whether she said "liberry" or "library," a conversation Keeba was all too happy to ditch.

"Hey, Kee. You dancin' or conversin'?" Arkim broke in.

"Dancin'."

Jekyll was hot, and amid the crowd Keeba and Arkim danced to a mix of Missy, Nas, Busta, and some old Black Rob. Then the slows came on. Not sure what to do, Keeba just stood. Arkim reached for her and she stayed with him through the love grooves of Jaheim, Mary J., even some

Mariah, and, at the very end, Usher. She felt Arkim's height, smelled his musky odor, tasted his lips. When the music stopped, they both looked down.

The next day the girls rose early, ate cereal, and headed out the door. "Bye, Ma, we going to work!" called Teesha, her words echoing as she and Keeba noisily ran down the stairs.

The salon still looked festive, but a few balloons had leaked air and begun to shrink and wrinkle. The main room reeked of paint. Keeba flung open the windows, careful to check for mice in the office before going in to open that window. Teesha used a brick to prop open the front door.

Keeba turned on the boom box Butta had donated from the Housing Authority's lost-and-found office and sat on a stool. Teesha went into the office and put the steel cash box Mrs. Washington had given her inside the desk drawer. On top of the desk, she lay a writing pad with two columns: "Customer Name" and "Amount." Next to the pad she placed two new pens, a pencil, a new Pink Pearl eraser, a wind-up clock, a pack of Trident bubble gum, and Arkim's Gameboy she'd borrowed. She sat listening to the clock's tick, Keeba's radio music, and traffic passing on the street. When it seemed like the clock had drowned out all the other sounds, she went to hang with Keeba.

Keeba was on the floor, her head against the wall.

"Why you down there?"

"Them stools hurt—you can't rest your back against nothing. Can't we get real chairs? I know we on a tight budget, but our clients gon' be cripple if they have to be perched up like that. Skye's friend was fidgeting and frowning the whole time I was doing her braids. But every time she saw me scopin' her in the mirror she would make her face be smiling—you know how they do, trying to act like everything's *honkie dorkie*, or whatever they be saying, even when their back be broke. White people funny."

Teesha leaned against the wall and slid down to the floor next to Keeba.

"Word. Let's buy some real chairs this weekend, after we make some money."

She played Gameboy. Keeba opened a bottle of gloss and painted her toenails. The woman from the Laundromat walked by and waved hello. A police car slowed down as it drove by. The cop in the passenger seat smiled and shook her head, her braids flying. A bald guy stopped in the doorway, rubbed his hand over his head, shrugged, and moved on. A pair of little girls with runny noses hopped through the doorway, screamed, "Teekee tookey dookeyhead!" and bolted, whooping and shrieking.

Teesha could still hear the clock ticking.

"It's almost lunchtime, Kee. Don't people need their hair done?"

"From all the peas in the kitchen and naps in the pantry I saw yesterday, I'd say definitely, and bad."

"Since they're all in denial, let's eat and come back later."

Later was just as quiet as earlier. Keeba did the Game-Boy and Teesha painted her toenails. People waved, smiled, looked, and kept walking. Teesha took from her desk a stack of flyers announcing the opening, with their home phone number "for appointments only."

"I bet Arkim didn't even hit every apartment, with his lazy behind," said Teesha. "That's why we don't have clients."

Keeba hadn't said anything to her sister about Arkim, figuring Teesha would make fun of her.

"I'm sure he gave them out. He wouldn't do us like that." What Keeba really meant was he wouldn't do *her* like that. "We got cheap neighbors, that's the problem."

For the rest of the afternoon and half the evening, Teesha and Keeba went from door to door, floor to floor, building to building distributing their flyers. Sometimes people congratulated them. Others said twenty-five dollars was too expensive, to which Teesha responded each time, "That price not for you—you my girl" (or "buddy" or "homey" or "man" or "godmom," depending on the person). When dogs barked, the sisters ran away screaming. Afterward, Teesha suggested they go to Brooklyn Heights.

"The liberry open this late?" Keeba hated walking when

she didn't have to and wasn't about to go all that way for nothing.

"Nothing but white people in the Heights and they *live* in libraries. So it should be open. Maybe we can put up some flyers there. What time is it now?"

The sisters hurried through the streets. They were crossing through a park separating the two neighborhoods.

"I'll ask this lady what time it is." Teesha took off to catch up with a woman strolling along a leaf-strewn pathway in heels and a leather coat. She was carrying a briefcase. "Excuse me . . . Miss . . . Miss?" The woman glanced over her shoulder and quickened her step as if she were late for a train. "Miss!"

Keeba found the scene funny. Teesha glared at the woman's receding back.

"What you running from, lady?! Nobody don't want you!"

Keeba recovered enough from laughing to shout, "Hope you fall on them stilts and twiss ya ankle!"

Teesha was disgusted. "Can you believe that? We supposed to be all united and patriotic, and white people still see black and panic."

"I *told* you that face could scare a little baby. Now if it had been *me* asking for the time—"

"She woulda sprayed ya big pieface with Mace!" retorted Teesha. She smacked Keeba's neck and ran.

They made it to the library shortly before closing. Skye was seated at the checkout counter.

"Teesha! Keeba! You made it!" She got up and came toward them.

"Don't get too excited—we didn't come for liberry books," said Keeba.

"Kee means not *this* visit. We came to . . . thank you for helping out at the opening and to . . . um . . . show you our flyers."

Teesha wanted to kick herself. Skye had *made* the flyers, so of course she had already seen them. Duh.

The librarian beamed. "Well, what a wonderful surprise anyway to see you both, and congratulations again on your fabulous opening day. My colleagues love my new look and a couple are interested in having their hair done as well."

"They white?" asked Keeba.

Teesha stepped on her foot.

"I mean, what kinda hair they got, the sliding kind like your friend's or, you know, thicker? My poor fingers need something to grab on to."

"All grades, Keeba. And by the way, Rae *loves* you, *and* her hair." A man with an armful of books appeared and Skye stepped away to take care of him.

Keeba said, "What's wrong with her? Who asked what grade they were in?"

Teesha started to roll her eyes but, remembering her

promise from that night before the opening, caught herself and stopped. Skye returned holding two books.

"I suspect you don't have your cards with you today, but I recognize you as new members. These are from our young adult section. Teesha, I think this title will appeal to you." She handed Teesha the thicker book. "It's the story of Madame C. J. Walker, an African American born in the 1800s on a Louisiana plantation. She invented a hair softener for kinky hair, founded a successful cosmetics company, and was one of the first American women to become a millionaire."

Teesha snatched it. "Really?"

"And Keeba," said Skye, "this one was written by a young woman raised in the projects who relies on her smarts and—this is where I think you'll resonate with her—her humor to surmount some pretty daunting obstacles and become a successful attorney."

"She rich too?"

"That I couldn't say for certain, but I didn't get that impression."

"So why *I* gotta get the poor one?"

Skye smiled. "I never said she was poor. Trust me, you'll like it. But, and this goes for both of you, you only get to take them out on two conditions: if you promise to return them on the due date so others will have the opportunity to read them, and if Keeba does me a favor."

"What?"

"Repeat after me . . . li*bra*ry."

Keeba repeated the word, dragging out the middle syllable as long and loudly as possible.

"Shhh," whispered Skye, looking around. "So anyway, how *is* business?"

Keeba said it was slow. Teesha said nothing.

"Don't go getting discouraged this early in the game, you two. It takes time to build a reputation and expand a client base." She looked hard at the sisters. "Do I detect an underlying motive for this visit? Yes, you *may* leave the flyers here. I'll make sure they're noticed. Now I better get back to work—the closing-time book rush is on." She lowered her voice. "Holler your way later, ah-ight?" Then she winked.

Keeba leaned toward the librarian and said in a very soft voice, "Ah-ight." She winked back.

The next day they had one client, and she wanted her hair done—but only if she could pay the old price of fifteen dollars. For the rest of the week they had four other clients. And no tips. The weekend came and buying barber chairs wasn't mentioned. Saturday, Keeba had two clients.

Sunday, the salon was closed, a relief to them both. They spent the afternoon in Toya's apartment. She showed them the salon Web site's new images from the opening, the links she'd set up with other black hair sites, and the hit counter that recorded the number of site visitors. Teesha asked about computer school.

"It's really hard," Toya answered, "and half the time I

feel like the teachers are speaking a different language, but I'm learning so much. Come to the living room and check out the digital photo montage I put together for my parents' wedding anniversary. You too, Kee."

"Nah, that's all right. I like cruising this Web site. But why you ain't put in my baby pictures I gave you?"

Teesha and Toya played with the digital camera, taking pictures of each other and deleting the bow-wows that didn't come out cute enough. When they returned to the bedroom to load the images, Toya did a double-take at their Web site.

"I don't know how you're doing it," she exclaimed. "Tee-Kee's had seven visitors, what, a half hour ago, and now there's twenty-five! Your site is drawing mad traffic."

"Oh, that was me," said Keeba. "I kept clicking it while y'all was in the living room so the number would go up and we'd look more popular."

"Awww," moaned Toya, holding her head.

Teesha couldn't contain herself. "Duh, duh, and duh. All for you."

"What*ever*. At least our Web site don't seem like some reject dot-com nobody wanna look at."

The next week was worse. On Monday, Aisha sent them her nurse friend, Miss Jane Constantino, a strawberry blonde whose fine hair could barely hold a braid. But Teesha liked her because she told crazy delivery-room stories and gave a big tip. But no one else came. Teesha and

Keeba took turns playing Gameboy. They flipped through their library books.

On Friday and Saturday the braid salon didn't open at all. Instead, the girls and Arkim papered their enemy project, Fort Crest Houses, with flyers. But by Sunday, Arkim had heard that some flyers were scribbled on with curses and insults about "Hillbilly Houses" and others had been burned off the walls.

In the middle of taping a Rap 'n Roll Miami commercial, Aisha's cell phone vibrated in her fanny pack. She made the hand signal for "cut."

"Yo, Peter, I gotta take this."

The director frowned. "It can't wait?"

"Nope. But you can."

He scowled. "Time's money, honey." But then he said into the megaphone, "Okay, people, ten minutes!"

Aisha skated off the set and plopped down on a floor cushion.

She recognized the caller's number. "Wassup, Tee!" she yelled. "I'm down in Miami getting jiggy widdit. How's my homegirls, y'all blowed up yet? I wanted to be at the opening real bad, but they had me way out in—"

"It's all good, Ai," Teesha cut in. "The first day was bomb—*everybody* came out. After that, business slowed down some, you know how it is. Thanks for the nurse— she was cool. But I gotta tell you straight up, TeeKee's need a *whole* lot more people, people with cash. You a star—can't you send over some celebrities? Alicia Keys has braids and Maxwell has cornrows in one of his videos. What about Terence Trent D'Arby, he's still alive, right? And Macy Gray need serious help; Keeba could work some *mad* braids outta that bouffant. White people are okay too. Hey, we'll even take them long-haired show dogs with the curly tails."

"Whoa, Tee, *simmah down nah*. I'm no star like *that*. You talkin' Humvee-driving, private-jet-flying, mansion-buying megastars. I do commercials for skating rinks. How I'ma know people like that?"

"Then what about some basketball players like, what's his name, the one always getting in trouble whose cornrows are always fuzzy."

The director was pacing. "Earth to Aisha! Time's money!"

Aisha said, "I gotta go, Tee—they giving me mad drama over here. I'll try, but I don't roll like that. Now y'all betta not be losing my hard-earned benjamins or I'ma hafta do a Tony Montana on your butts. Say hello to my little friend!"

Teesha tried to laugh. "Be cool, Scarface, or we'll have to call in the Cleaners."

"Ah-ight Tee. Holla atcha."

When Teesha hung up, Mrs. Washington said that was the longest two-minute phone call she ever heard. "When the bill come, make sure you check off all your calls."

Keeba had been holding her fingers crossed for good luck. "So what she say, what she say?"

"Don't worry," Teesha said. "She's sending some good-fellas over to adjust our joints."

As week after week passed, and things didn't pick up, TeeKee's Tresses was open less and less often. The sisters braided the same few heads that they had braided before going into business. Once in a while a boy would want his rows touched up. But the money that had been plenty when there weren't expenses to pay was no longer enough.

8

Butta wasn't far from the truth about the folks in Water-front. While four hundred dollars a month felt like robbery to project residents with little income, it seemed like chump change to professionals sick of paying a thousand bucks for a studio. But they weren't the only ones checking out the low rents and free utilities of public housing and licking their lips. City officials worried that big-time professionals might move someplace cheaper, and take their cash with them.

The only people happy about rising rents were private landlords. But out in Seaview, a gated community on the edge of Coney Island, Sal Boberri was feeling quite unhappy about one of his properties. He banged on his messy desk, stirring up a cloud of dust.

"What the . . . Who on earth is Edwina Washington and

why am I getting checks from her?" He pulled more mail from beneath the coffee pot. "Shirley! Get in here!"

A petite woman with tightly curled white hair sauntered in.

"Find out what's going on at 155 York. I got headaches up the kazoo already without folks playing musical chairs with my properties. And for crying out loud, don't throw mail on my desk!" He pointed to a plastic tray stacked to overflowing. "Can you read this? It says 'In Box.'"

"I know. It's the in box, though, not a file cabinet. Go through your mail once in a while, Sal, and it wouldn't build up."

The secretary pulled a dog-eared copy of the Brooklyn white pages from the coat closet and took it to her desk. She read down the list of names under "Washington." Within minutes she was dialing the number for "Washington, Edwina P."

Keeba reached it first. "What?" she said into the receiver.

Mrs. Washington shouted, "Keeba Washington, you know better than to answer the phone with no manners!"

Keeba chuckled and started over. "'Scuse me. Hello. What?"

"Good morning," said a woman's voice. "Is this the residence of Edwina P. Washington?"

White. Plus, nobody said "Edwina P." Keeba wasn't about to let no white saleslady bother her mother.

"What you want? Who's this anyway?"

"Pardon me. My name's Shirley Elf and I'm calling with regard to 155 York, which—"

"Ohhh, you want a appointment!" Keeba's face brightened as though a gleam of sunlight had broken through a cloud bank and was shining directly on her. "You have to 'scuse me, Miss Elf, I'm evil when I first wake up. This Kee, Keeba Washington, one of the . . . uh . . . bosses. I'ma be the one doing your hair. You want twists, rows, extensions, or braids?"

The conversation continued, and Keeba wrote Shirley Elf's name down in the appointment book that was kept next to the phone. She even gave the caller the salon's Web site address and said good-bye politely.

"You sure changed your tune on *that* call," Mrs. Washington said afterward. "Who was it?"

"A new client. Some white lady Skye musta sent us. And *I* scooped her right up—I smelt benjamins through the phone."

"You shouldn't be competing with your sister like that, Keeba. You know you had somebody last week and she had not a one. It's good you girls are putting all your income together, but the tips are separate and Teesha needs some too. She over there right now sitting and waiting, and you up here swishing around in your pajamas."

"What*ever*. Tee the one cash-crazy. I just want a little spending money. Destiny's Child is my role model: 'I'm a survivor! I'm gonna make it! I'm a survivor! I'm gonna take it!' "

"The Lord's my role model and greed's ungodly."

Keeba leaped from the couch. Throwing air punches, she jabbed, flailed, and ducked as if fighting a swarm of flies.

"What? What? Bring it *on*, Edwina P., bring it *on*, 'cause I floats like a butterfly and stings like a Kee!"

Mrs. Washington watched her daughter hop around, wear herself out, and collapse on the couch. Then she calmly walked over and sat on her.

"Owww! You breaking my ribs, Ma! I can't get no air! Ahhhh! Help!"

"Who's floating now, Miss Survivor? You gonna stop hogging clients?"

"Okay, Ma! Get *off* me! I'ma share! I *am*!"

Mrs. Washington took her precious good time. "I knew I raised a generous, sweet child."

At last she freed her daughter. Keeba lay still, moaning dramatically.

Sal Boberri leaned over Shirley Elf's shoulder, squinting through his glasses at the computer screen as the secretary pulled up TeeKeesTresses.com.

"Wouldya get a load of this? Place used to be one of those Spanish bodegas selling green bananas and six-packs. For *years*. A crappy storefront I got for a few bucks and made some good money on. Now it's a fancy beauty parlor run by a couple of ghetto kids. With a Web site, no less! I'm a hardworking businessman and *I* don't even have that."

"That's because you're too cheap to pay for one."

"Click on the home page again. Look at that crowd! I tell ya, these gals gotta be *rolling* in dough, knowing how the blacks are with their hair. Remember when they all had those Afros sticking out to there? The barbershops must've been going *nuts*."

"I remember your curly hair got pretty long too, Sal, before it all fell out."

The landlord took the mouse and clicked from image to image. Skye March addressing the crowd. Teesha and Keeba dancing. Church members clapping. The TeeKee's Tresses sign. Keeba braiding artist Rae Brock's hair. The framed photo of Aisha Ingram.

He put his finger on Aisha's face. "You gotta be kidding me. That's that kid from the TV commercial." He clicked to enlarge the image and read the inscription. " 'To Tee and Kee, my homegirls 4 life! And ya *know* dat! Love, Ai.' Zowee, Madames Tee and Kee travel in hotshot circles! Look around this office, Shirl—I own half of Brooklyn, but do *I* have autographed pictures from the rich and famous?"

"You don't need pictures—you have half the city council over to dinner every other week."

Sal Boberri was a big campaign donor to any local

politician who promised to "advise" him on obtaining city-owned properties going into foreclosure.

"You wanna know what gets me, Shirl? I'll tell ya what gets me—and don't take it wrong: I'm doing business with these people for thirty years, got nothing against them. It's the *squawking*, the *griping*, the *whining* . . . These guys just don't quit. The overpriced supermarkets, the welfare cuts, the low wages . . . They even sued Pizza House for not delivering to the projects after dark. Gimme a break—the delivery guys wanted to live! If ghetto life's so rough, how do these gals have computers, Web sites, and rich friends? I betcha anything they have a Mercedes parked behind that little beauty parlor."

"You have two in the driveway."

Sal clicked back to Rae Brock. "A white girl in the projects . . . *That's* a hopeful sight. Think of the *fortune* we'd make if the middle class could buy into low-income areas like they did in Waterfront, fix up the neighborhood, and rent space from the Boberri Group for their outdoor cafés, sushi joints, and vitamin stores. They'd have affordable housing, the city'd be free of a million headaches, I'd get a fair return on my holdings for once, and everybody wins. Fuggedaboutit—I'd even buy *you* a Mercedes."

"Then I'll be driving one in my grave," Shirley said drily.

Boberri walked back to his desk, still talking.

"I gotta give 'em credit, though—it's a shrewd scam. Take over the lease. Say nothing to the owner. And pay bodega rent for luxury salon property. I tell ya, it's always the same attitude: 'Dupe the white guy, rip off the honky.' Well, we'll show them what this white guy's made of, won't we, Shirl?"

"We always do."

"Type the letter."

The day of Miss Shirley Elf's appointment, Teesha was in a hopeful mood. Skye had apparently kept her word to send them library clients. Kee had passed the woman to her "in the family spirit," she'd said. And from the way things sounded, this new client had money. TeeKee's Tresses had been open for a few months, their loan money was shrinking, and not much was going into the cash box. Teesha had a feeling. Maybe Kee wasn't just tripping when she said this lady might be a "good-luck elf."

Keeba was comfortably propped on a giant beanbag chair with the book (whose due date was long past) from Skye. Teesha sat on the wooden desk chair she'd taken from the office, watching the door. The heat was turned up high and the front windows were sweating. The clock ticked.

"It's a quarter to eleven. I thought she was coming at ten."

"She is," responded Keeba, absorbed in her book. "This chick is *out* there, but she got heart."

"Then where she at?"

"I'm up to the part where she moved to Seattle because

she hated the law firm where they had her working like a slave."

"Not *her*," said Teesha. "I mean the *client*."

The door opened, ringing the bell above it. It was only the mail delivery.

"Good morning," said the uniformed woman, looking around the empty salon. "Looks like you ladies need to advertise. Registered letter for TeeKee's Tresses, care of Keeba and Teesha Washington. Either one of you can sign."

"I'll take it," said Teesha. "What kinda hair you got under that cap?"

"A perm. Have a nice day, girls, and good luck."

Keeba turned her attention back to the memoir.

Teesha ripped open the envelope from the Boberri Group and read it, and then reread it.

When the silence got to Keeba, she looked up. "What?" She could tell from her sister's face that the news was not good. She put the book down.

"I can't believe this! The landlord trying to say Miss Henriquez rent don't apply to us since we not on the lease."

"What he talking about? We paying the rent, right? So what*ever*! How much they want? Four hundred's too much as it is, for this lil' bit of space."

"*Double*, Kee. Or they're going to put us out and padlock the gate." Teesha burst into tears.

Keeba rushed to her. "Hey, come on," she said, putting her arms around her sister. "We ain't come this far to end up out on the sidewalk. Things'll work out."

"But how?" cried Teesha, almost pleading. "How *things* going to work out when we need *twice* as much cash as we *didn't* have in the *first* place? We don't even have new clients."

Keeba had no idea how they were going to manage, but all she cared about at that moment was making her sister feel better. "You know how Ma's always talking about the darkness before the light? So we got bad news. I still feel like today's appointment might bring us luck."

"Oh, you mean the lucky elf? *She's* the one who signed this piece of paper."

Keeba snatched the letter. At the bottom was stamped "Shirley Elf for Sal Boberri."

"*That's* who called the house!" raged Keeba, crumpling up the letter and throwing it on the floor. "I'ma yoke her. We ain't paying nothin'! I'ma *yoke* her!"

Sniffling, Teesha took Keeba's wrist. "You're not yoking nobody. Or you'll be locked out *and* locked up." She suddenly felt as if she were suffocating. "I gotta get out of here."

The sisters shut down the heat, turned off all the lights, locked the door, bolted the security gate, and left. With most of the loan money still in the bank, Teesha had worried more about finding new clients than keeping the salon open. Now she had to face the fact that the rent increase put the very existence of TeeKee's Tresses in danger, and sliced in half the time they had left to bring in more business.

Had they been too ambitious, project girls imagining they could own a business, blow up, live large? She'd heard the haters' mumblings, seen their smirks. *Tee act stuck-up now. Kee think she all that. Their ticky-tacky salon ain't going nowhere.* Aisha was doing great, so why not them? Well, maybe there was a reason why not—maybe the lucky elves blessed only one project girl, and Aisha was it. Maybe there was no more luck to go around.

Mrs. Washington's reaction went from bemused to biblical. "What in the name of . . . How they expect poor people to come up with double the rent . . . *eight* hundred dollars?" She bowed her head, said a prayer, and then looked up at her daughters. "If He brings you to it, He'll bring you through it."

Dinner was a glum affair. The church woman tried in vain to make Keeba and Teesha see the possibility of a hidden blessing in what looked to them both like an outright calamity. Keeba's anger, like a brush fire, seemed to burn away all that she ate, causing her to devour one portion after another. In contrast, disappointment so filled Teesha that it left no room for food. She excused herself from the table and took refuge in her bedroom.

9

*B*utta took the steps three at a time, to the fourteenth floor, his Knicks warm-up suit drenched with sweat in spite of the brisk temperature. Determined to stay fit no matter how steadily age was creeping up on him, he'd put in his hour of early-morning hoops. Inside the apartment he rubbed his knees, ruined doing high jumps on concrete courts, and stretched out his back, wrecked pushing heavy mops on hallway floors. After his usual cold shower, he downed a bowl of oatmeal, pulled on a blue custodian shirt and matching pants, and left for his job at the Housing Authority office.

At the same moment, in a vast apartment overlooking the Brooklyn Botanic Garden, Councilman Jerry Mudd was holding his coffee cup aloft for Mrs. Mudd to refill.

He felt like he hadn't slept at all and was still exhausted from the previous day's work. A council debate during which he was repeatedly interrupted, an elders' luncheon where he spoke before dozing seniors, afternoon meetings with demanding constituents, and a dinner at the home of a wealthy supporter that went way too late. And now he had to drag himself halfway across the city to some god-forsaken public housing project. It was a good plan he'd devised; he just wished he could set it in motion from the comfort of his breakfast nook. At times like these, he wished he'd gone into business like his dad instead of public service. He beeped his driver to bring the car around.

The massive trees of the projects shook their browned leaves to the ground. On their way to school, children with heavy coats and plaid knapsacks kicked apart the piles Butta had carefully raked together. Normally, he would've chased them away and rebuilt the mounds, but he was in the supply room searching for more Hefty bags. A voice from the adjoining office caught his attention.

"This is how it would work, Fred. Hillbrook would be the test case. We sell off the three- and four-bedroom apartments to outside people with money, offer current residents the smaller units at cost, and the whole neighborhood blossoms from the cash infusion. Better maintenance, better services, better schools. Totally win-win. Feel it out for me—you know people in the Waterfront district, take their pulse. Between you, me, and the wall, I'm looking into this strictly as a favor for a buddy, a big money guy out there in Seaview who remembers his friends around election time. No, the mayor's not in on this one, which is better. But I'll propose it to him if there's a chance it'd fly."

The conversation shifted to lovely wives, soaring tuitions, overpriced stocks, and the councilman's swank new health club that he never had time to go to. After staring for a while at the wall as though he could see through it, Butta grabbed the rake and left without the bags.

The librarian and the custodian collided in the lobby of their building, she rushing to work and he racing to his telephone.

"Sorry, Butter! You all right?" Skye March's shoulder bag had slammed into Butta's midsection.

"Damn, girl, what you got in there, cement blocks? Good thing I got the real abs of steel."

"Books. And I'm really sorry. But you ran into me. Where's the fire?"

Butta shook his head, nodded, then shook his head again as if he couldn't, yet could, believe what he'd heard. "It's gon' be everywhere when I bring to the people what's going down. Ain't gon' be about next time—prepare for the fire *this* time."

"Butter, have you given any thought to poetry? You've got the abstruse part down. What are you talking about?"

He repeated the conversation he'd overheard, about

Housing's plan to sell Hillbrook Houses. "The man gon' kick out folks with large cribs and sell 'em to them frontin' yuppies from the water's edge over there. The rest of us get the studios and mini-cribs, that is, if we got the bucks. That's how he divides and conquers, by controlling supply and demand. Nobody can't tell me the government ain't elbow-deep in this, FBI, CIA, the whole apparatus. You watch, Fort Crest will fall, then Farragut, Marcy, Red Hook . . . Sister Angela broke it down back in the day when she said they coming in the morning for us first, but that's only the start. See, that's why that chump J. Edgar tried to silence her on some trumped-up charge that she smuggled a weapon in her Afro when everybody who got hair know for a fact—"

"You're losing me here," Skye butted in. "Can we stick to the present? If what you're saying is true—"

"The truth is always true."

"All right, then it's true. And I'm flabbergasted. It isn't possible . . . not New York . . . not today. Pardon me for rambling, but I'm completely shell-shocked. Okay, focus, Skye, think. First thing we do is bring everyone into the loop, let the tenants know. This calls for a preemptive strike."

That made Butta grin. " 'Preemptive strike.' I like that, guerrilla commando tactics. I'll go make some calls right now."

And so began the campaign to save Hillbrook Houses. The librarian examined old Housing Authority building plans in the library's archives and calculated that 65 percent of the apartments consisted of three or four bedrooms. They'd been built to accommodate what the documents described as "the typically large families of the lower income classes." And Rae Brock canvassed her fellow Waterfront co-op owners to get a sense of what "at cost" might mean for a modest apartment in an area such as Hillbrook. She learned not only that more than half of the current residents would be squeezed out but also that the remaining ones would never be able to afford their apartments under the councilman's plan.

That Sunday Pastor Phelps stepped up to the pulpit and contemplated an ocean of faces, familiar ones that he'd watched age over the years and new ones he had only glimpsed here and there in the neighborhood. He adjusted his glasses, bowed his head, and said the opening prayer. Then he addressed the issue that had brought more residents to the Church of the Open Heart than he'd seen in years.

"As I look out upon you, I see women and men, young people and children, families who have lived here in Hillbrook for thirty, forty, even fifty years. *Generations* of good, hardworking project folk. Folk like our young sisters back there, Teesha and Keeba Washington, whose beauty parlor they're trying to shut down by doubling the rent. And why? Because they don't want us to form our own companies, have our own businesses, succeed on our own terms."

"I hear that!"

"They got *no* love for us!"

The minister continued. "Now they want to be our neighbors. But I ask you, brothers and sisters, did *they* want to be here with us when the jobs left?"

"No!" answered an old woman in the first pew.

"No, they did not. Did *they* want to be here with us when the drugs arrived?"

"No!" shouted voices from both sides of the room.

"No, they did not. Did *they* want to be here with us when parents grieved and diseases thrived?"

"No!" cried the whole church.

"No, they did *not*! So why . . . why in the name of *God* . . . do they want to be with us *now*?!"

Responses came from all over.

"They devils!"

" 'Cause they know the terrorists ain't after *us*!"

"To spy!"

"So we'll show 'em how to dance!"

The young pastor laughed. "I see some of *you* should be up here. Or maybe onstage at the Apollo." There was boisterous laughter. "I'll tell you why, my brothers and sisters! Because for the first time in their cushy little lives they're getting a *taste* of what we have been *chewing* on for *decades* . . . the crumb of poverty." He bowed his head.

"Preach, pastor!"

"Amen!"

"Break it down, brotherman!"

Pastor Phelps raised his eyes and his fist hit the pulpit with a loud bang. "The boomers are *broke*. The dotcommers are *destitute*. The privileged are *po'*. But we an *angry* army, a *mighty* multitude, a *fierce* flock! And we will *not*, I repeat, *not* . . . be moved. Brothers and sisters, go on back to your homes. You know what to do. God bless."

A roar of amens shook the windows. With Toya singing the lead, the gold-robed choir broke into the gospel anthem "I Shall Not Be Moved." Butta sang in a deep, booming voice. Skye followed along excitedly, flubbing the words but clapping in beat as hard as she could. Next to her, Rae smiled and hummed. Behind them, Mrs. Washington was singing and elbowing Tee and Kee, who were dancing as if in a nightclub, as was Arkim. Children, grownups, and teenagers raised their voices in a great music to let the heavens know that, like a tree planted by the water, they would not be moved.

TeeKee's Tresses bustled with activity. Packets of leaflets were being distributed, posters stenciled, instructions given, calls made, tea poured . . . and the day was just beginning. Pastor Phelps's sermon and the fear of being forced out of their homes had fired up Hillbrook. Aisha was expected to show up, and Raven promised to hop the train as soon as she finished her last exam for the semester.

Keeba was gluing pictures of Madame C. J. Walker in a white shirt and long black skirt to a cardboard sign reading "TeeKee's Tresses Walks with the Best." She and Keeba planned to carry it on the march Butta and Skye had organized. Hillbrook residents were going to cross the Brooklyn Bridge to the Housing Authority's headquarters.

"Courtesy of the copy center," said Skye, handing a stack of leaflets to Mrs. Washington. "Give one to everybody, Sister Washington, even the joggers on the bridge."

A pair of carefully made-up teenage girls were having their hair done. Teesha was working on one and had persuaded Toya to do the other.

"You can keep the tip," Teesha whispered to her friend.

"Tip?!" exclaimed Toya's client, overhearing. "Uh-uh, that's out. I'm paying what it cost and that's *it*."

Rae had had her cornrows redone for the occasion. She was on her umpteenth phone call.

". . . Yes, at *least* five hundred marchers, maybe more"— an exaggeration, but the point was to make it sound interesting—". . . That's right . . . On the bridge at noon . . . That's exactly it, public housing on the auction block . . . Yes, the real estate slave trade . . . I like that. Good, see you on the bridge!" She slammed down the phone. "We got one! *Brooklyn News* is sending a reporter!"

All morning the salon continued to buzz with people who were helping out, sharing stories, giving advice, or simply hanging. Mrs. Washington gave Tee her pocketbook to lock up in the office.

One person stood out from the others, not because of any physical difference but because of her attitude. She'd ease in, stand around watching, then walk out. Sometimes she'd be in the doorway of Teesha's office, peeking in. Other times she'd linger near conversations, listening but not participating. Then she'd loiter at the door of the supply cabinet idly playing with the key in the lock.

"Who's she?" asked Rae.

The room was packed and no one caught Keeba's eye. "She who?"

"Her, the one with the red headband and red bushy hair. What a rich color."

Keeba looked the girl over. "Somebody whose hair hurt my eyes," she said, and didn't give the girl another thought.

But the redhead was on *someone's* mind because her cell phone rang. The girl hurried across the street and sat on the back of a bench.

"What they doin'?" asked the caller.

"Gettin' ready, making posters and banners and crap."

"I'm *glad* Hillbilly Houses gettin' dogged. I hope the cops beat they asses *down*."

"Some white lady trying to get them on the news."

"Man, they so *drama*. Nobody give a damn 'bout tacky TeeKee's. Do it look like we can get in?"

"No sweat. The window on the side don't got no bars, no alarm, nothin'."

"Cool. We gon' yoke 'em and smoke 'em, then."

"All the way."

"I be down later, Red."

"Ah-ight, Shaniq. I'm out."

10

A blustery wind from behind propelled the marchers forward as they climbed the promenade steps. The continuous drone of six-lane traffic filled their ears. Bikes sped in both directions, rumbling noisily over the walkway's wooden slats. Draped from four suspension cables was a lace network of steel wire rope. Rising in the distance like great cathedrals were the dramatic twin arches of the bridge's Brooklyn and Manhattan towers, each one supporting an immense American flag. The blue space in the sky where the city's other twin towers had once stood caught the eye of many as they pressed on, determined.

Numbering close to fifty, the marchers waved banners and signs, and stuck leaflets in the hands of curious tourists and hesitant onlookers. People smiled at the churchy women in wide coats and thick shoes, who looked old enough to be veterans of the 1950s integration struggles. Some onlookers stepped back, though, when Butta, wearing sunglasses, a black beret, and Army fatigues, approached with his petition.

But it was the teenagers who drew the most attention with their ghetto glamour and Fifth Avenue attitude. The girls were flawless. Smooth hair glistened, finely woven braids blew back like streamers, and bleached blond Afros adorned heads like golden bouquets. Colorful leather bomber jackets and booty-tight jeans gave them the allure of female hip-hop stars. A few were listening to portable CD players. The boys, wearing tight doo-rags under backward FDNY, NYPD, and FBI caps, were somewhat hampered by the gusty wind's effect on their baggy pants. But they strutted and fronted with style, rocking oversized denim jackets from Sean John and vast thick sweatshirts from Phat Farm. The one homeboy still in Tommywear was dogged so badly that he went home to change.

Keeba was peering down, gripping Arkim's arm.

"Look, you can see the water between these planks! They better be solid. I can't swim!"

Next to her daughter, Mrs. Washington took a peek, shut her eyes, and mumbled, "He walketh with me."

Skye looked down at the roiling river. "I wouldn't worry, Keeba, the boards are an inch and a half thick, and no one's crashed through yet over the past hundred years."

"A inch and a half?!" Keeba squeezed harder. "Can't you walk faster?"

Teesha, holding a sign with one hand and her mother's arm with the other, wanted to know how high up they were. Skye knew almost everything about the bridge since part of her duties as a librarian was to take calls from the public on the information hotline.

"Actually," Skye said, "we are exactly one hundred and thirty-five feet above the East River."

"Oh shi—" Teesha started to say. Her mother shot her a warning glance. Mrs. Washington didn't put up with cursing. "Oh snap! Me and Kee been up here a lot, but I didn't know it was *that* high up!"

Back on the street, Aisha nearly banged into a wall while swerving into a parking spot at the entrance of the bridge. Strapped in on the passenger side, Max gave her the sideways eye.

"Baby, driving isn't like skating. You can't turn and spin anywhere you choose."

"I know, I know. But this is an emergency. They trying to evict me and my moms. Driving rules is suspended."

They dashed up the steps to join the protesters.

Leading the march, Butta tried to get a chant going. "No justice, no peace! No justice, no peace!" He was walking backward, facing the marchers. "Come on, everybody, make some noise! Let the man know we on the move! No justice, no peace!"

But the crowd was feeling more playful than political,

cheered by the sunshine and buoyed by a belief in their own power.

"Oh please, nobody got shot!" a woman yelled. "And you need to pull your little tilted tam down on *both* sides before that bald head freeze!"

Laughter rolled from the front to the back of the demonstration like a human wave at a baseball game. Butta raised his fist. "That's all right, y'all can clown now. But remember . . ." And like a choir soloist he sang out, "The people, united, will never be defeated! The people, united, will never be defeated!"

They arrived at the concrete span on the Manhattan side. Rae didn't see any reporters. She looked hopefully toward a taxi that screeched to a stop. Raven jumped out and ran to join her neighbors. Rae called the *Brooklyn News* guy on her cell phone but got no answer.

The Housing Authority's headquarters were on Broadway, directly across from City Hall Park. As the group crossed the street, stopping traffic and distributing more leaflets, a police lieutenant approached with raised hands.

"Whoa, slow it down! Hold it right here, folks! This area's off-limits to pedestrian traffic!"

The project people came to a stop and gathered around. Skye, seeing Butta move toward the cop, rushed over. "Good afternoon, officer," she said. "We're going to Housing Authority headquarters to deliver a petition."

"I'm sorry, miss, but like I said, the zone's closed. We got an official ceremony going on at City Hall for the

Trade Center site and a lotta important people are down here."

"We're important too."

"Nobody's saying you're not important, but I'm sorry, I still can't let you through. Now if you folks'll just clear the area . . ."

Pastor Phelps, clasping a Bible to his chest, led his church members to the front. "Sir, I have brought my flock from the Church of the Open Heart in a spirit of nonviolence to stop the theft of Hillbrook Houses from the people who live there. Reverend King said—"

"I know, I know, everybody's got a gripe. You have a permit, Father?"

"Officer, the Almighty *himself* . . . permits our protest. The King of *all* kings . . . sanctions our struggle. The Lord of this *life* . . . authorizes this assembly."

"Amen!"

"Praise his name!"

"Hallelujah!"

"Folks, please, you must disperse!"

An Asian officer joined his lieutenant. "Move it back, people, move it back!"

The officers eased forward with outstretched arms.

Butta stepped up. "Yo, my man, lemme get a word with just you. I know *you* know what time it is, my brother. My people picked the white man's cotton, your people built the white man's railroads—"

"You're thinking about the Chinese. I'm Japanese."

"That's okay, my man, we all in the *of color* crew. Hiroshima woulda *never* went down like that in a white—"

"C'mon, wise guy." The lieutenant had had enough of Butta. "I'm asking you nicely to turn your people around . . ."

Wise guy? That was Butta's cue to lead his comrades across the park and into struggle. He raised his leg to step over the barricade, but his knee gave out and he lost his balance. The Asian officer, who was closer than his colleague, moved to catch him, but Butta crashed to the ground.

"Oh snap," he said, chuckling and struggling to his feet, "I played myself."

Standing in the middle of the protesters with his view partially blocked, Arkim saw something else. "They got Butta! He's down!"

A stunned groan grew into a bellowed chant. "No justice, no peace! No justice, no peace! The people, united, will never be defeated!" Journalists nearby heard the noise and, deserting their posts at the official ceremony, raced toward the commotion, trailing mikes, cameras, and tripods.

Nudged away from Centre Street by a quartet of mounted police, the Hillbrook residents held a full-scale news conference at the entry to the bridge, denouncing the city's efforts to oust them from public housing. Pastor Phelps preached to the camera next to Butta, who struck a militant pose with his arms folded on his chest and his face in a scowl. Aisha held forth about project girls being kicked to the curb like in that old movie *Set It Off*. Raven recounted her journey from teen pregnancy to college. Skye explained to a reporter why a middle-class librarian who could live anywhere opted to "go project," while behind her, Rae slid into the frame of the camera shot to display the Web address on her T-shirt, artworkswithin.com. A cameraman liked Keeba and Teesha in particular and zoomed in on them repeatedly as, together, they held up a sign and tossed their braids. When the last reporter asked a final question and walked off scribbling on a pad, the happy marchers headed for the subway and rode back to Brooklyn.

No one ever would have imagined what awaited them back at TeeKee's Tresses.

At the same moment the lead marchers were on the bridge's wooden walkway, Shaniqua Page and her homegirl Red were breaking into the salon. Using the brick doorstop, they shattered the office window and climbed in.

"Let's show 'em how we do!" cheered Shaniqua. In the main room, the first thing that caught her eye was the photo of Aisha, her former romantic rival.

"Oh, ain't that *sweeeet*?" she mocked, pulling it down. "*Moooo* . . ." She flung the frame against the wall. "You got a lighter?" Red tossed her a New York Liberty cigarette lighter she'd found in a purse she'd snatched as a woman was leaving the basketball game. Shaniqua held the photo at arm's length, flicked the flame, and watched Aisha's face blacken, curl, and crumple into a charred pile of ashes. "Rest in peace, cow."

Red ripped down the celebrity pictures. "Like anybody famous would ever come in here!"

Standing on each side of the supply cabinet they tipped it forward. Onto the floor crashed combs, brushes, packs of hair, shampoo, conditioner, shower caps, rubber bands, string, scissors, tools, hand mirrors, notepads, and towels, all of which they ravaged however they could.

Shaniqua beat Keeba's radio to smithereens with a hammer. She hurled the batteries at the front windows, rejoicing as the glass exploded against the salon's closed metal gate.

Going back into the office, she set upon Teesha's desk chair with fury, slamming it around but with no result. Enraged, she found a saw among the tools Arkim had left there and sawed apart the desk, leg by leg. Her arm began to ache, a pain that reminded her of the soreness she had felt after the scuffle with the Washingtons during that project party back in the early summer.

"Hey, Red, let's start a campfire!"

Red said maybe they should chill on that. The fire could spread.

"I don't care if I fry up *all* these Hillbilly suckers, *and* that creep Kevin." Thinking of how Kevin had dumped her for some new hottie on the block, Shaniqua let her attention bolt from fire to furniture.

She began snatching drawers out of the desk and dropping them. The last drawer was locked, but didn't stay that way for long. Breaking it open, she found a scruffy pocketbook and a cash box. "We got bank!"

Red ran into the office and helped Shaniqua jimmy the lid off the steel box with a crowbar from the stash of tools. They mocked the amount of money inside.

"They ain't even getting paid," gloated Shaniqua.

"Losers," said Red.

Red went through the pocketbook. First she found a checkbook. Then she felt a lump inside the lining. "A wallet!"

"They mine," declared Shaniqua, "the checks and the wallet. You keep the cash from the box."

Shaniqua's heart pounded as she panted from the effort of her destruction. "Watch this, Red!" Wielding a leg from the wooden desk like a baseball bat, she returned to the main room and pounded the large wall mirror, sending shards of glass all over the place. In her frenzy she didn't notice that a sliver had nicked her finger, drawing blood.

Red pulled a switchblade from her pocket and snapped it open. "Where y'all gonna sit ya big butts now, TeeKee?" She plunged the sharp knife into the padded seat of one stool, then the other, slitting open the fabric covering and tearing out the padding with her hands. Throwing it into the air, she screamed, "It's raining cotton!"

Still they weren't quite finished. Shaniqua and Red sweated and strained their way through stripping the paper from the bathroom walls and ripping out the electrical sockets. Whatever could be splashed across the floor, they splashed; whatever could be burned, they burned; and whatever could be wrecked, they wrecked. Then they left the same way they entered, through the jagged office window. Shuddering with rapture, they rushed from the alley and darted into the street, crossing the path of a Mercedes-Benz. The sedan slowed to let them by, and the girls disappeared between the towering buildings.

11

The Hillbrook tenants embraced at the subway station and went home in the evening darkness. Mrs. Washington was too tired to go to the salon. She reminded Teesha to bring her pocketbook home.

Back at TeeKee's Tresses, Teesha turned the key in the padlock and started raising the security gate. She felt hopeful and confident but mostly proud—of her sister and mother, Pastor Phelps, Skye, Butta, her friends, everybody. They'd *done* it. The march had been a success—Butta had tripped over his own feet, but it was a lucky accident that had gotten people to listen to them, and they had made themselves heard. Keeba was right, things would work out. The gate slid up.

"Tee!" Keeba said from behind her sister. "You *know*

you s'pose to leave a light on. I hate walking in here in the dark."

"I *did* leave it on."

Keeba stepped on something. "What's this?" Broken glass was on the sidewalk. "Look, Tee, the front window's broke!"

Teesha unlocked the door and the sisters stepped inside.

The street lamp lit a scene neither could quite take in. They stared, blinked, stared some more. A tornado had torn through the salon. At least, that's how it looked. They couldn't speak. They couldn't comprehend. They stared.

"Oh my God," breathed Keeba.

"I-I'm gonna th-throw up," stammered Teesha. "Call the cops."

The police took pictures, dusted for prints, collected some bloodstained glass, and interviewed other shopkeepers in the neighborhood. They wrote down the girls' statements and said they'd be in touch if anything came up. That night the Washington family cried and talked and cried some more. Mrs. Washington called Skye to come over, and the four of them cried again. They sat close together discussing, brooding, searching.

No one had a clue at first, but as they went over recent events, an answer hit Keeba like a lightning bolt. "The elf!" she cried.

Mrs. Washington sat upright. "What elf?"

Teesha smacked herself on the forehead. "Keeba's right, Ma," she shouted. "It has to be the elf."

"Is this some kind of collective breakdown?" asked Skye, looking from one girl to the other.

"The lady who called here to make an appointment," Keeba explained. "Shirley Elf! She truly gettin' *yoked*!"

Teesha was absolutely sure that her sister was right. "It's the landlord. They don't want more money, they want us *out*! I bet it's part of the co-op thing."

The women talked late into the night. By morning, the lead story on the local news channels was "The Hillbrook Heist," a reference that exasperated one news watcher in particular—the mayor of New York.

Mayor Colton Modiano had been fielding calls from reporters all morning and by now he was fuming. He gave his aides their orders with wrathful precision. There would be a full written report on the combined fiasco of the coverage of the march and the story about the break-in at the salon that very day or it was Jobs.com for the whole pack of them.

In the meantime, he had to quell the panic that was spreading throughout the public housing system and spawning copycat marches in every borough. So he called his own news conference. And the salvos flew.

"How long has this plan been underway, Mr. Mayor, to oust the poor from the very neighborhoods they were dumped in precisely because they *were* poor?"

"What is your comment on charges that this administration is willing to dispossess low-income blacks and Hispanics to make wealthy executives happy?"

"Is the city's war on poverty in reality a war on the poor?"

"Are there rogue elements in city government, Mayor Modiano, affiliated with white supremacist groups?"

The more the mayor explained that neither he nor his administration was aware of or would support any such proposal, the louder the cries of cover-up. There were calls for his resignation.

A few hours after the disastrous news conference, a knock sounded at the door of the mayoral office.

"What, goddammit?!" barked Modiano, a typical greeting from the famously bad-tempered mayor.

Deb Jones, a junior aide, braced herself and entered. "I'm here to brief you, Mr. Mayor, on the Hillbrook Heist."

"Don't say that! I forbid you to use that ridiculous expression in this office! Heist, my ass. The media are sensationalizing the heck out of this story. Do you know there are more than three hundred housing projects throughout the five boroughs? I had never even heard of this Hillbrook place before yesterday, let alone planned to sell it. Now sit the hell down and tell me what you've got."

Deb Jones had almost fallen off her love seat the night before when she saw her old Vassar roommate Skye March on the evening news. She had tracked her down easily, first thing that morning. Skye had put Deb on to a real character named Butta, who had sent her to a Fred Earnell in the housing office at Hillbrook. But this wasn't the time for self-congratulation. She knew to cut to the chase.

"Mudd did it. The councilman from Brooklyn's thirty-fifth district. He contacted a constituent named Fred Earnell, whom he'd helped find work at Housing—a low-level paper-pusher job—with a scheme to take Hillbrook private. Earnell says the conversation was purely exploratory. But I got him to admit that Mudd wanted it kept secret, especially from you, sir."

Sitting low in his leather swivel chair, turned to face the window, the mayor listened, fidgeting with a letter opener. Deb Jones watched her boss's ears change color, a sight that always made her stomach hurt.

"It's all in here," she concluded, carefully placing the report near his appointment calendar.

Mayor Modiano spun around red-faced and big-eyed. "Jerry Mudd?!" He stabbed the letter opener into the report. Jones leaped backward. "You see to it that schmuck's in my office first thing in the morning!"

"Yes, sir," Jones said hastily, and fled.

* * *

When the unpopular councilman left Mayor Modiano's office at noon, pale and perspiring, an aide snickered, "Mud pie, anyone?"

A news release went out that afternoon "From the Desk of Jerome F. Mudd III" describing the public servant's "bold, personal initiative to find innovative ways to expand the available stock of affordable housing for middle-income New Yorkers." The media ignored it, the Hillbrook Heist already yesterday's news.

The Robbery Unit detective listened politely to the allegations against Sal Boberri. He questioned whether the pieces really fit together as perfectly as the Washingtons thought. When landlords destroy their own property, he said, it's to collect insurance money. And they usually burn it down to the ground. The crime scene in this case didn't fit that profile. He said he'd check out the lead anyway.

Hillbrook's residents needed much less persuading.

"They want war, then bring 'em war."

"Flip 'em the clip, special delivery, that's all."

"Get word to Clinton up in Harlem—he down with us."

Outrage in the Waterfront area ran as deep. Skye let Rae know what had happened and the artist was immediately on the phone with friends.

"That kind of thing is *so* September tenth!"

"I thought stuff like that only happened in the movies!"

"The gallery's *got* to do a fund-raiser for those kids."

People who had never even hung with the sisters called

or dropped by their apartment to give a shout and tell them to keep their heads up. Arkim took Keeba to Coney Island.

The Washingtons' home phone rang nonstop. The first callers offered sympathy and support. There was Aisha's mother. "Thank you, Louise," said Mrs. Washington, "and I sure will let them know Ai said she's on the case. Starlett and Ty okay? . . . Oh yes, I *do* hope one day I'll be blessed with grandchildren."

Raven's mother called. "That's so sweet, Gwen, but no, we have plenty food. When you talk to Raven, say Sister Washington thinking about her. And kiss little Smokey for me. He still climbing walls like Spiderman?"

Then Toya's mother. "His ways *are* mysterious, Sister Larson. Remember us in your prayers."

Strangers called too, people who'd seen Keeba and Teesha on the news and wanted hair appointments. Mrs. Washington wasn't sure what she should say. She didn't want to tell them all that TeeKee's Tresses was no more, but she also knew how hard the girls had tried to get new clients. So she said the salon was temporarily closed for remodeling and took people's names and numbers. Maybe that list, getting longer and longer, would cheer her daughters up some.

"Why you do that, Ma? There *is* no salon," complained Teesha one day when she heard her mother take such a call.

"Yes there *is*, or there would be if you would stop mop-ing around, and go down there and fix that place up. The church is ready to help, your friends are ready . . . You're doing exactly what that man wants—giving up."

"You ain't *seen* it," said Keeba, "stuff poured out on the floor, nothin' *not* broke up."

"Okay," said Mrs. Washington, grabbing a broom, a dustpan, and her coat, "then take me to see it."

Keeba and Teesha knew better than to argue with their mother when her mind was set, so they grabbed jackets and followed her out. Mrs. Washington's first stop was the church, where she rounded up whoever was sitting around in the Senior Center. Armed with mops, buckets, and sponges, they found Butta on his break and got him to come along and bring his equipment. As the cleanup crew crossed the projects, it picked up some of the homeys loitering in lobbies and hooky players hanging in halls. Teesha raised the security gate and that day, as well as every day for the rest of the week, they cleared away, swept up, washed off, painted over, and rewired TeeKee's Tresses.

At the end of it, there were still no mirrors, stools, or pictures, nor was there a desk, chair, clock, or radio. But the dented supply cabinet was standing upright, and they'd salvaged some scissors, a package of blue rubber bands, and a few hair extensions that hadn't been torn to bits. The walls were a fresh apricot color and the floor had been repainted dark gray. Part of the front window was taped over with cardboard, and a piece of wood had been nailed over the hole where the office window once was.

"Nice," Keeba said with a smile.

"Um-hmm," agreed Teesha, surveying the space. "Guess we're back to zero, except with higher rent. Think anybody will take over the lease?"

"Tee, you know Ma don't want us goin' out like that. Look at the girl in the book I read—all kinds of bad stuff happened to her but she got it together."

Teesha primped her lips. "That's her. But did *she* have a braid salon that got demolished when she already couldn't pay the rent?" Keeba was forever dreaming when she should be scheming. The end of the month was a few days away and they needed so much money it wasn't even worth adding it all up.

"Noooo," countered Keeba, "but she ain't give up on what she *did* have, a dream to be a lawyer. What about your idol, Madame C. J. Walker? You said she was a cleaning lady, then came down with high blood pressure. But she stayed on it, going door-to-door selling hair grease. And when she died ain't she had a Harlem mansion straight outta *MTV Cribs*?"

"So? That's *her* too. Now stop irking me."

"F'git it then. G'head and mope. The space still look nice."

They waited. No client appeared. No clock ticked. No postal worker dropped in. When it seemed like maybe they should just go home and hope for either a call from the detectives, a visit from Madame C. J. Walker's ghost, or a simple miracle, there was a knock. Both girls almost jumped out of their skin.

Rae Brock's face appeared at the window. Kee let her in.

"You guys are incredible, look at this place! From what Skye had said, this was a federal disaster site."

"It *was* mad wrecked," said Kee, "but folks came through for us big-time."

Rae examined the room, nodding her approval. Then she asked, "Can I say something without you taking it as a criticism?"

"What?!" snapped Keeba, placing herself toe to toe with the artist. "Don't *make* me get out this car, white girl."

A flush of color spread into Rae's face.

Teesha cracked up. "You so *crazy*, Kee. Don't pay her *no* mind, Rae."

Rae tilted her head to one side and stood nose to nose with Keeba. "*Brake* yaself, sucka!"

Teesha's eyes bucked. Keeba dropped to her knees and then fell backward on the floor, wailing with laughter.

"You crazy too, Rae," said Teesha, trying to compose herself. "Where'd you get that?"

" 'Don't Be a Menace to South Central While Drinking Your Juice in the Hood.' *The Wayans Brothers*. It's hysterical." Rae went on to say that, since "discovering" the projects, she'd tried to learn more about this world only a few blocks from Waterfront but galaxies from her awareness.

"The Wayans *are* real funny, especially the sister," agreed Teesha, "but to learn about the projects maybe you should check out stuff on a Web site or at the library, you know, something more, I don't know, dignified."

Keeba wanted to know what Rae had come by to say.

"That the pink color you guys had painted this place with before was *really* bad. This color's so much better."

"What*ever*!" Keeba said.

Rae then handed Teesha an envelope. "This is from the Waterfront Artists Co-op. We had a fund-raiser so you could buy some more of those uncomfortable stools."

Teesha slowly opened the envelope and pulled out a check for a thousand dollars. She showed it to Keeba. They hopped around, grabbed Rae, and hugged her between them.

"See, Tee, I *told* you!" Keeba shouted.

Teesha saw.

Keeba insisted on tightening Rae's braids, an offer the artist gladly accepted.

At last, with no other clients and with exciting news to tell their mother, the Washington sisters closed the salon for the day.

"You ain't gonna believe this, Edwina P., but we got a thousand dollars! Show her, Tee!"

Teesha displayed the check. "For the salon. The Waterfronters collected it for us."

Mrs. Washington's face beamed.

"Well, bless their hearts. I got news too, and it's just as good. They found my ID!"

The girls screamed.

"The detective called and said a girl went in the check-cashing place in those projects over near the expressway—"

"Fort Crest?" asked Teesha.

"And she tried to cash one of my checks. The people called the cops and they picked her up right there. She had my wallet too. No money in it, of course."

Keeba frowned. "How some Fort Crusty skank get . . ." Her eyes met Teesha's and she fell silent.

"Prayer is powerful," declared Mrs. Washington. "Let's go to the precinct."

The detective was solemn as he handed Mrs. Washington her wallet. "You're lucky. The kid wasn't too bright. Thought she could write herself a fifty-dollar check on a stolen checkbook and cash it at a legitimate establishment. The lab's matching her fingerprints against the prints from the scene. But when you got a public place like a hair salon with people coming and going, it can be a problem. We think she's the one, though. Any questions?"

Keeba and Teesha elbowed each other. Teesha spoke. "Who was it? What she look like?"

"Like you gals. Braids. Only blond." He flipped open a file. "A . . . Sheeka . . . Shanaka . . . Page. Fifteen years old."

Keeba started coughing so hard the cop had to give her a little paper cup of water. Shaniqua wasn't no fifteen!

"We're verifying the suspect's age."

The sisters grew quiet, cutting their eyes at each other. No way they could let on that they knew her. Otherwise, the party, the fight, the smashed aqua blue punch bowl . . . It would all have to come out. So on the way home they pretended to marvel along with their mother that "a mere child would do such a terrible, terrible thing."

Behind the closed door of their bedroom that night, Teesha and Keeba debated whether to tell Aisha.

"But you know how she can go *off*. She hate Shaniqua anyway," said Keeba.

"I know," said her sister, "but it's her salon too when you calculate in all the cash she put up. She's the owner in a way."

Aisha *did* go off when they called her late that night after Mrs. Washington was asleep. But then she calmed down and said that since the skank was already busted, she wouldn't have to bust her up herself.

The salon's lack of adequate supplies and furnishings was eased by the gift from the artists' co-op. But there remained the problem of head traffic. Initially, a stream of income flowed from the Waterfront artists who went in for purple braids or a trio of red-white-and-blue twists or green cornrows. Unfortunately, the novelty clients who wore braids a short while for fun but never returned for a touch-up, tightening, or new style didn't offer the steady repeat business the salon needed. Not surprisingly, the stream slowed to a trickle and eventually dried up.

"Ai sent me" was on the lips of a string of hip-hop and rap fans from Rap 'n Roll rinks. More demanding than the Waterfronters, they nonetheless gave few tips.

Mrs. Washington finally suggested contacting the people whose numbers she had collected during TeeKee's "remodeling." Maybe they still wanted appointments. If there's such a thing as mother's intuition, Mrs. Washington's suggestion was its prime example. A dozen callers became clients and kept Keeba and Teesha twisting, tucking, and tying for days.

TeeKee's Tresses wasn't exactly Grand Central Terminal, but the salon's new, steady client base gave the two owners enough income to enroll in an evening program at the Madame Walker Beauty School. When the idea for opening a business had begun—back while talking to Skye on the benches—becoming licensed beauticians had seemed like something beyond the sisters' reach. Now it was just around the corner.

Keeba was spending a lot of time with Arkim, which seemed to please her mother and not to displease her sister. Teesha, in fact, preferred her sister to be with Arkvark, a nice if Urkelish project boy, than with some lame "keepin-it-gangsta" thug. One evening, he was waiting when the young women came out of the beauty school.

"Hey, baby, what you doing out here so late?" Keeba

gave her boyfriend a peck on the cheek, too self-conscious to really kiss him in front of Teesha.

Teesha, quick to notice the absence of Homey and the presence of a new shirt on Arkim, raised her eyebrows. "What, the big dawg without his little dog? Whoa! And why you sporting another woman on your chest when you got Queen Kee?"

Arkim's jersey featured L.A. Sparks superstar Lisa Leslie.

" 'Cause Number 9 got mad game, even though she is female."

"Right, Ark, like you don't notice how pretty she is when she goes up for a dunk." Teesha still couldn't resist teasing him.

Arkim smiled. "It ain't even 'bout that."

Keeba showed him her fist.

"Listen up y'all," said Arkim, changing the subject. "I was hangin' with Kevin and he said Shaniqua's last court date's tomorrow. She's been back and forth, getting adjourned a million times like they do people, but this is the real deal. I been letting people know. We going too, right?"

Having been released by the police into her mother's custody, Shaniqua had spent a lot of time in her bedroom lately. "Fort Blunt HQ" read the graffiti on the door. She was holed up with Red, who'd been living with the Pages since her moms threw her out for pulling a knife on her brother.

Shaniqua's mother, with her ever-changing boyfriends, came and went on an irregular basis. Sometimes she and one of the boyfriends had to lie low for a few weeks while some double-crossed dealer hunted them. Other times they'd burst in breathless and sweaty, fresh from a robbery, and stay for a day or two.

Tonight, Shaniqua was busy choosing what she'd wear to court the following day.

"How this look?" she asked Red, who was sitting on a pile of dirty clothes watching television. Shaniqua stepped on empty Chinese food containers and kicked aside crushed beer cans as she strutted her dark gray Rocawear baggies and red tank top.

"You phat." Red was just sixteen and already a professional booster. Her skill at stealing clothes from department stores and selling them cheap to her neighbors had earned her outstanding warrants for grand larceny and possession of stolen property. So she didn't dare show her face in court for her friend's sentencing, which made her feel guilty.

"You know I'd be there tomorrow if the heat wasn't sweatin' me."

Shaniqua shrugged. "Ain't no thang. I know you holds me down when you can. I'ma walk anyway—they got nothin' on me. I found that lady's stuff in a paper bag in the trash can. So what if I tried to cash a check? As far as they know"—she laughed—"that's my first offense. I gets to keep walkin' like Johnnie Walker Red."

The girls high-fived each other, confident and fearless.

"Word. You prob'ly be outta there by lunchtime, so lets hook up at Catfish Corner. They ain't gon' be able to hold you. Nobody seen you nowhere near that joint."

Red was relieved that Shaniqua wasn't worried about the possibility of doing time. Sometimes people crack and start naming names so they can cut a better deal with the prosecutor. With her outstandings, Red knew the cops would love to get their hands on her.

Across town in a tidy neighborhood of elegant brownstones and luxury cars, Ashley and Jesse Honoré were whispering beneath the high ceiling in the living room of their spacious home. Their parents were out of earshot in the salon enjoying martinis on the rocks with some lawyer couple. But still the brother and sister whispered.

Jesse was adamant. "You can't just do nothing. This is important. Suppose me and Raven had gone back early to wait for the others, like we almost did, because she was tired. Somebody could've been hurt—cut, shot, anything."

"That's why I was driving by in the first place. I thought everything might be over and you'd be back there. But instead, I saw her coming out of the alley alongside the salon with some marginal-looking redhead. I should have done a public service and run them both over, but Dad would've killed me if I'd dented his new Mercedes." Ashley looked down at the tray on the coffee table, impaled an olive on the end of a toothpick, and ate it.

"This isn't a joke. You have to go to the hearing tomorrow and tell them what you saw. She could go free and try to get more revenge on Keeba and Teesha—"

"Those names . . . ugh!"

"Or anyone else who was at the party, including you. You heard what she said—'Payback's a bitch.' "

Ashley ran her slender fingers impatiently through her fresh perm. She no longer bothered to whisper. "You know what your problem is, Jesse? You're too involved with these people. They all have major issues. I couldn't care less about their ghetto warfare and ghetto blasters and ghetto Cheetos parties! Get some perspective, for crying out loud. Mom's a judge, Dad's a school principal, I'm a Columbia B School student, and you should be concentrating on your future. You want to know what the real bitch is? Failure, Jesse. Failure's a bitch. I thought you were marrying *one* of them, not the entire tribe!"

"Man, screw you, Ashley!"

Hearing the raised voices, Mrs. Honoré excused herself to her guests and entered the living room.

"Silence! Court is now in session!" The courtroom buzz quieted only slightly. Family, friends, and curious spectators filled the benches. Overworked legal aid lawyers met clients for the first time; harried prosecutors quickly familiarized themselves with charges, rap sheets, and community reports; and the lone private attorney checked her watch repeatedly.

Keeba and Teesha were in the third row, flanked by Mrs. Washington on one side and Arkim on the other. Next to them sat Skye, having taken a personal day off work: Butta, who was "reporting for duty to monitor the system"; and Pastor Phelps, appearing on behalf of the church's Teen Outreach Program (TOP), which had a branch in Fort Crest Houses.

"All rise, the Honorable Judge Betsey Kennedy presiding!"

A handful of people stood up while the rest continued to eat snacks, mumble into cell phones, and flip through the *New York Post*.

"All rise!" bellowed the bailiff.

Handcuffed teens were brought in one after another from the holding pen. Stripped of gangsta wear and repackaged in prison gear, they looked like what they were—scared, angry children.

"Docket Number 186, *State* vs. *Bert*, speeding, reckless endangerment. Docket Number 191, *State* vs. *Byrdsong*, insurance fraud, theft of medical services, resisting arrest. Docket Number 290, *State* vs. *Laverte*, possession of a dangerous animal. Docket Number 810, *State* vs. *Perdu*, arson, weapons possession." In and out of the dock they paraded, getting adjournments, taking deals, or pleading not guilty until their lawyers prepared arguments for reduced charges, extenuating circumstances, or decreased bail. Unnoticed, Shaniqua Page slipped into court and took a seat at the back of the room.

The Washington sisters joked about how clumpy people's hair became after a night or two in jail. Skye and Butta talked quietly with the pastor, all three of them grim-faced. Mrs. Washington and Arkim watched.

"Docket Number 69, *State* vs. *Page*, breaking and entering, aggravated vandalism, grand larceny, check fraud, possession of stolen property."

Alone, Shaniqua walked slowly past the rows of benches, her eyes straight ahead. She pushed open the swinging wooden dividers that separated the officers of the court from the spectators, and stopped. She had had a different lawyer with every court appearance, and today she recognized no one. She walked toward the one she thought might be her defender.

"Over there, kid," said the prosecutor, indicating the other counsel desk.

"Mr. Lewis," warned the lawyer representing Shaniqua, "I believe that's an ex parte contact. I urge you to address me, not my client."

The two lawyers, friends from law school, eyed each other amicably.

"Give it a break, Kristy," said Mr. Lewis. "You dealing?"

"If I may have a moment to consult with my client . . ." Shaniqua's lawyer glanced through a file and then turned to the girl. "Did you tell the arresting officer you were fifteen? According to your school records here, you'll be eighteen in a month. Trying to outwit the system isn't going to please this judge—she's one of the toughest. You have some pretty heavy charges against you, which means you are potentially facing serious time. As I tell all my clients, with your authorization I can cut you a deal right now. I recommend it. The court always rewards accuseds who don't clog up the docket with multiple appearances and lengthy trials. I don't care whether you did it or not, that's not my role to decide. But if the prosecutor wins at trial . . . and the evidence is there . . ."

"Ain't no evidence nowhere! I didn't do nothin'.'"

"Look, don't waste my time, Page," said the lawyer. "The fingerprint analysis was inconclusive, but a witness places you at the scene."

"Nobody saw me, that's bull, you can't railroad me."

The judge gestured to the lawyer to speed it up.

"Just a moment longer, Your Honor." The lawyer brought her mouth closer to Shaniqua's ear. "Does a gray Mercedes-Benz sedan refresh your recollection? The driver spotted you and a redhead fleeing the scene, okay?"

The lawyers huddled, conferred with the judge, and stated for the record that Shaniqua Whitney Page agreed to plead guilty to simple vandalism and petty larceny. Judge Kennedy sentenced her to thirty days in a women's detention facility, to be followed by six months of probation, community service, and mandatory counseling at TOP.

Meanwhile, Red waited outside the fish restaurant for

an hour before spotting one of her other homegirls in a stolen car and jumping in.

Sal Boberri hadn't enjoyed being interviewed by detectives. He needed people sniffing around asking questions about his business like he needed a hole in the head. Next thing you know, you got the IRS paying you a friendly little visit. Once things quieted down with that incident at his York Street property, he discreetly sent the Washingtons a second registered letter. It contained a new, three-year lease in the name of TeeKee's Tresses. There was no mention of a change in the rent.

A celebration was in order. Mrs. Washington cooked the girls a big dinner of beans and rice, barbecued spare ribs, collard greens, and, for dessert, a double-layer coconut cake.

"From the lips to the hips," boasted Keeba as she ate her second slice. "I gotta fill out."

Teesha poured herself some ginger ale. "Ma, please tell your child that if she fills out any more, the arms of that chair she's squeezed into are gonna snap off."

"What*ever.*"

"You two will never change will you? The more grown you get, the less growed up. Pass me the soda." Pouring from the plastic bottle reminded Mrs. Washington of something. "Sure wonder what in the world happened to my punch bowl."

Her daughters exchanged looks.

"You must be getting that Oldhimey disease that make old people forget things," said Keeba.

"Yeah. I bet it's in a closet somewhere. You look in the clothes closet?" asked Teesha, biting into a juicy rib.

"Of course I didn't! Who gonna put a punch bowl in with clothes? I was sure I put it in the cabinet."

"*Was* sure," Tee said. "Life's hard on the elderly."

Mrs. Washington threw her napkin on the table. "Miss know-it-all knows it all." She went to the closet, opened it, pushed coats this way, choir robes that way, and . . .

"Well, blessed be . . . Knock me down and fan me with a brick! Here it is!"

12

It was a Sunday afternoon, which normally meant the salon was closed, but the lights were on and music was playing inside.

"Not there, Ai. Terence Trent D'Arby's played out. Put me next to Usher!" Keeba waved Aisha to the opposite wall, where Teesha was hanging a glossy photo of Usher, leering in black leather and gold jewlry. Aisha stepped heavily from the footstool and rolled her eyes hard.

"You need to chill with all that bossin' me around, Kee. First you want to be up with Alicia Keys, then it's 'No, she so cute she make me look ugly.' Next you want to be with Missy now that she's all slim and got her new braids. Then you're all like 'Terence look GOOD!' Now it's Usher. I ain't gon' be climbin' up and down all day, wearing down my ankles that I need for skating."

Keeba was happy. She and Arkim were getting along great. She had a job doing something she liked and was good at. And she loved her mother and sister more than anything. Money was tight and she knew that worried Teesha, but things were going to work out . . . she just had that feeling.

Aisha crossed the room carrying Keeba's framed Madame C. J. Walker Beauty Course Completion Certificate bearing the graduate's smiling face.

"That's word," said Arkim, sweeping bent nails, crumpled shopping bags, and balled-up snack-food wrappings into a pile. "Usher ain't got no braids anyway, so why he on the wall at all? If y'all gon' do it like that, put me up there."

Toya was sitting on the floor separating packages of hair by color. "Sounds to me like somebody's jealous."

Arkim shoved some trash her way.

Teesha jumped down from her stepladder. "Hold up right there, Aisha." Like a prosecutor arguing a defendant's crimes directly to the judge, she didn't look at her sister. "This wall is my wall. Kee got her space, I got mine. She got her diploma, I got mine. Now, when we were downtown at the Fulton Mall, I asked her if she wanted this Usher photo and she said no . . ."

"Tee don't even lie! I said I wanted it, but didn't have enough money 'cause I had already paid for my other ones before I saw that one!"

Toya and Aisha were already laughing out loud. Arkim

shook his head. Skye listened intently with a faint smile on her face. Teesha continued as if Keeba hadn't said a word. "So I said, all right, but don't get in my face about it when we start decorating the salon. So to make a long story short, my wall, my Usher, my face squeezed up nice and close to his." She fluttered her eyes and made a loud kissing noise with her lips.

Aisha turned around and shrugged at Keeba. "Sorry, Kee. Look like Tee gets to hang beside your man."

Keeba took her diploma and placed it on her wall, opposite the Usher poster. "What*evuh*! That's ah-ight anyway 'cause she just next to him like a side order. But who he got his eyes on? Me! So squeeze up to *that*, sista-girl."

Toya laughed herself red-faced, looking down from one sister to the other. "Can you just explain one thing to me? Since when do people even put their face on a diploma? Y'all seriously bugged."

It was Keeba's idea to tape photos of themselves over the drawing on the certificate. The picture didn't represent TeeKee's right, she said, because the woman's hair fell to her shoulders in a swirling perm and their salon was about braids. Besides, after the hours they'd had to put into learning permanent waving, chemical relaxing and press-ing, chemistry and cosmetology, thermal curling and a lot of other stuff that had little connection to what they'd do at the braid salon, the sisters were feeling pretty rebellious. There had been state laws to learn, sterilization techniques to study, razors, clippers, scissors, and thinning shears to master. So in a sense they'd earned the right to have their own faces on their school certificates. No, they would not put that blow-waved, bleached, and frosted woman up on their wall. In her place were Keeba and Teesha, grinning and coiffed on their school certificates.

"I must say, your degrees did look a little strange to me as well," said Skye, "but I just assumed it was the school's way of affirming the students' visual identities since cosmetology is a visual discipline."

The teens cut each other looks as if to say, Uh-huh, yeah, right.

At the same moment, an imposing man wearing sunglasses and long, black braids under a cowboy hat walked into the salon.

" 'Sup?" said the man.

Skye was the first to peer a little closer. "Is that . . . ?"

"Why y'all gotta be dumbstruck like you ain't never seen a brother from another planet who's down with Milli Vanilli?" He raised his hat, and with it came the fake braids sewn into the headband.

Keeba burst out laughing so hard it sounded like she was screaming. The others followed.

"Butta, you a crazy dude!" shouted Arkim.

Skye's face was streaming tears. "The braids are fetching, Butta, really fetching. But you see what happened to that pop duo with their fake braids. I wouldn't be so eager to model myself on them."

"Hey, they just took their reserved spot in the dustbin of history." Butta laughed too. "I just wanted to give y'all ya props for taking the fall and rising on up. Bam! This is how we do it. Blackatcha, all the way."

Skye got that quizzical look on her face that meant she didn't understand a word Butta was saying. But Project Sphinx, as she called him in her journal, had grown on her. She was even considering inviting him to dinner one evening.

Maybe.

The friends hung out talking about the wild ride they'd been on together. The joyous opening day, the protest march, the vandalism, the artists' co-op gift, the political scandal . . . they talked like veterans of some great civil rights struggle, when in fact they were just neighbors fighting for the survival of a shabby little beauty salon, but one that was theirs and of which they were very proud.

TeeKee's Tresses already looked like a business that had seen much better days, which was ironic given the short time it had actually been in operation. Despite the second-hand chairs, donated floor lamps, and the makeshift desk the Washingtons had built by laying a plank of wood across two rows of stacked cinderblocks, the place seemed absolutely bare. Which was the reason the girls had decided to cover the walls with celebrity posters and photographs, make the salon "more client-friendly," as Teesha put it.

Teesha knew they had to focus on bringing in as much

business as possible. The money from the artists had saved them as far as getting the basic supplies, but there were still rent, utilities, and other expenses to pay. Clients were coming in but not in the "living large" numbers she'd hoped for. It was going to take much longer than she thought before she'd have the cash and cars and fancy toys that had filled her fantasies. Then again, sometimes it seemed like they were fine just as they were. She was a high school graduate who'd started her own business. She got to work with her sister instead of for some stranger. And her job was in her own neighborhood, where she knew everybody and had lots of friends. They were already living large, just by living on their own terms.

"Oh, gimme your pie-face certificate," she said to Keeba, holding out her hand. Keeba immediately pulled the frame off the wall, where she'd put it next to a poster of Chris Tucker and Jackie Chan.

"I knew my sister wasn't evil enough to break up a happy home."

Teesha hung it and leaned away from the wall.

Toya tilted her head this way and that. "Move Kee's just a drop to the left." Skye suggested that Teesha raise her own certificate "a tiny centimeter."

Aisha thought the three frames should touch.

Arkim simply watched.

Butta said it looked perfect the way it was.

After a little more haggling the pictures were up, the Washingtons' framed certificates side by side, and the slick photo of the singer centered underneath them. Indeed, it *was* perfect.